Hustling on the Down Low

Hustling on the Down Low

M. T. Pope

www.urbanbooks.net

Urban Books, LLC
300 Farmingdale Road, NY-Route 109
Farmingdale, NY 11735

Hustling on the Down Low

ISBN 13: 978-1-62286-560-4
ISBN 10: 1-62286-560-X

First Trade Paperback Printing July 2017
Printed in the United States of America

10 9 8 7 6 5 4 3 2 1

Distributed by Kensington Publishing Corp.
Submit Orders to:
Customer Service
400 Hahn Road
Westminster, MD 21157-4627
Phone: 1-800-733-3000
Fax: 1-800-659-2436

Hustling on the Down Low

M. T. Pope

"The trouble with loyalty to the cause is that the cause will always betray you."

—*Transformers: Age of Extinction*

Acknowledgments

First, to God be the glory for the great things he has done.

Trying to sum up what I went through writing this book would take a book to explain . . . lol. Let's just say it was a roller-coaster ride. One day up and another down. If you are reading this, I finished the book. This is one that I hope you will enjoy as I do with all the selections that are released through me. This is my seventh full-length novel and a slightly different type of read.

Again, I want to thank my biological family, spiritual family, and literary family, all of whom have given me the push that I need to survive and thrive in this life. Thanks again for taking a chance once more on M. T. Pope.

Prologue

Corey

"The choice is yours," I heard my father speak. His voice sounded louder than normal, and it echoed throughout the room that we were in. I looked at him in his eyes and knew that he was serious. Very serious. I looked over at Dre, and my heart sank. His hands and legs were tied to a wooden chair. We were in the small room with two of my father's men standing in two corners of the room with my father in the middle close to Dre. I was against a wall with my body positioned toward them and the only door to the room. There was only one sound in the room that I heard, and that was the beat of my own heart. I was speechless. I didn't think that I would ever get caught. Now, here we are. I sat freely, unlike Dre. My father paced around Dre with a gun in his hand. All I could think about was the worst thing possible. Dre dying right in front of me.

"I can't believe that my own flesh and blood was a dick and ass chaser. Here I am doing all that I can to provide for you and your mother, and this is what I get as a reward. A fucking faggot. You had me fooled." He slapped Dre in the head with the gun, causing blood to splatter and run down his face. Dre didn't show any signs of weakness, though. He didn't budge at all. He looked at my father in the eyes the whole time. There was no sweat covering his face. No trembling or any such thing. He was the soldier that he portrays himself to be.

"And this was the piece of shit that you were sleeping with the whole time underneath my nose. You were supposed to be my right-hand man, and here you are dicking down my son, my own flesh and blood. You had me fooled. You had us all fooled. You all were fucking like rabbits, and then sitting at this table like all was right in the world. The ultimate betrayal in my book. I'm looking for a gay drug dealer with two right in my face." He then spat in my face. The hate was real on his face. I was no longer his son right now.

"As I said before, the choice is yours. You are going to choose your boyfriend's fate. A slow death or a quick one?" He looked at me, and then at Dre. Chills went down my spine. But I didn't show the hurt that I felt on the inside.

He then walked away from me and over to the table where a cooler was sitting on top of it. My mind raced with curiosity of what was in the cooler. It seemed like it took him forever to open the top to reveal what was inside.

"Here, we have slow death." He held up what looked like a syringe with blood in it. "This is a fresh dose of slow death or what is known to most as HIV."

My heart sank once again.

"Now, how do you want your boyfriend to die? His death is in your hands."

Chapter 1

Avery

Trophies

There was a cold silence in the room. Only the breath that entered and exited the bodies of those in the room could be heard. Fear had made its way in the room as well. I sat in the shadows and spoke from the darkness that covered my identity. Several other people were in the room, but they were irrelevant now. We were at a secret location that was in the middle of the city; out in the open but very well hidden. Fear was in his eyes. He knew why he was here. We all knew. One would think that my reputation for the ruthless acts that I've dealt out would speak for me, but there was always and always will be a nonbeliever. Someone to try your motherfucking hand.

See, they knew that I was gay and proud of it. They called it a weakness. *Sissy, faggot, come catcher, shit chaser:* those were the nice names they called me . . . us. I lived with it, thrived in it even. They were just names. They had no idea what it was to live in my world. They didn't care. Just call it a name and hope it goes away. Yes, those names hurt before, but I was numb now. Like I said before, they are just names.

So, this straight guy in front of me came in under the guise of a flaming sissy. I had to admit that he played the part well. He must have watched hours of *RuPaul's Drag Race* and the likes of it. One flaw, though. He wouldn't take or give up the dick or ass. He was close, but his ass bowed out at the last minute. See, to be a part of my crew, you had to be a top, bottom, or versatile. Gay was a must to be with me. He almost made it. I let him float around like I usually do when new recruits come into the fold. Let them get familiarized to their new environment. Then they must prove themselves. No, they didn't have to kill anyone . . . at first. But they had to be good in bed in their prospective positions in bed. At the least, they had to give good head. This guy couldn't and wouldn't do either.

When I first had my suspicions, I put him in the room that I use for testing a person to see if a person is who he says he is. You can't fake being gay. Putting them in this situation only has one of two outcomes. Either way, I loved the show and got some good nuts out of the positive outcomes, which were most.

In this scene with the infiltrator I had in front of me, I had him sleeping in a room that was his own "private room." I had one of my guys that was very easy on the eyes go into the room while he was asleep and seduce him.

I watched as the scene played out.

My boy crept in like the pro that he was, stark naked and ready for whatever, even an ass whipping if that was what it came to. My men were loyal and ready for anything.

There was sound being recorded as well for my pleasure. I wanted to experience it all. Sick bastard, you say. Yes, that was me.

The guy was asleep in the full-size bed that was pushed against one side of the room, wearing only a tee shirt and boxers. His body was spread-eagle on the bed as if he was at home. He snored and grunted in his sleep.

My boy eased onto the bed with him. He didn't even flinch. I watched my boy crawl on the bed and immediately went for the guy's dick. I watched as he reached his hand into the boxers and began to massage his manhood with his mouth. I was hard and horny just watching as it all played out. He feverishly began to go up and down on the guy's dick. Then dude woke up. He popped up out of the position he was in and then began to beat my boy like a savage. I had men posted on the outside of the door waiting for my cue if the situation went left. In this case, it did. I signaled them to go in and break up the situation, and that is how I ended up with this guy standing before me.

"Who do you work for?" I asked him in an even-toned voice. He was already scared. I didn't have to push him to fear me or the situation.

There was silence on his part. He was an average-built guy, not too heavy or thin, and he was very easy on the eyes. The person who sent him thought that we were as superficial as many gay men lead folks to believe. They were wrong. Dick and ass had no face, and most men would fuck or be fucked by anything that could pleasure them. Most lied and said they had standards, but they didn't. Many would let you poke them in any hole, including a nostril.

Anyway, since he didn't want to talk, I motioned to my men a signal that they all knew. They began to fully undress him. I had some big brute gay men on my force, but he didn't care. He fought even though he was thoroughly outnumbered.

When my guys first brought him in the room, they threw him into the middle of it.

"All of y'all are just a bunch of faggots." He then spit at one of my men. It infuriated my guy, which caused him to step to the phony. The guy positioned himself to fight.

I smiled from the shadows. I loved fighters that I knew were going to lose in the end.

"Take your best shot at this faggot." My guy taunted him like he was a bull. The guy didn't hesitate and threw a blow that landed and could be heard. But my guy didn't even flinch. Instead, he laughed.

One of my other men repeated the last scene with the same results, leaving the guy baffled and angry, so he charged one my men, and then the inevitable happened.

One forceful punch to his midsection and all his fight abruptly ended. I watched in delight. Two of my men held him up as he was now dazed and weak. He was naked, and his head hung low. He was now silent.

"Lift up his head," I instructed one of my men.

His eyes were glossy and struggling to focus, but he tried.

"Are you going to answer me, or am I going to have to persuade you?"

Spit laced with blood flew toward me but fell just before reaching me, giving me his answer. I was seething on the inside, but I didn't let it force me to respond. I just reached for the remote on my desk that opened a secret compartment in one of my walls. It was my "trophy case."

I pushed the button and watched as it opened and revealed my cherished collection. I let the doors open fully, and then I spoke.

"Sit him in the chair and turn him toward the wall."

His eyes were now fixed on the dozen jars that were on my mantles. Six large jars sat on each mantle with dates written underneath them. I smiled. They brought me great pleasure to look at them.

"Bring one close to him so we can see if he can guess what's in the jar." I motioned to one of my men, who carefully retrieved a jar. I saw the horror and fear cover his face instantly. His reaction was like most. First, he lost his bowels, and then he collapsed. My men hoisted him back to his feet. He was now willing to talk. But it was too late. He took the assignment to try to infiltrate my business, and there were always repercussions for actions. They say life is a gamble. I had the dice, and he was out of luck.

I pressed the button on my remote to release a screen from above, and then one of my men hooked up the video of the hour. I loved this video. We all did, but there was one person in the room that wouldn't enjoy it at all.

I pressed PLAY and the movie began. The sobbing began, and then the crying. This wasn't the sound from the movie, though. This was live theatrics from my latest infiltrator. Then there was the sheer shrieking of his voice that let me know that he knew his fate would be sealed. You see, I was a special kind of maniac. I wanted you to remember me for a lifetime. So early on, I enlisted the services from one of Baltimore's best plastic surgeons, one who happens to be gay, and brought him on my team. He showed up when I called without hesitation or fail. He was very good at what he did, and I had the proof on my mantles, and pictures too.

"You see, I hate wasting a good piece of dick, and God surely blessed you in that area." I looked at his plump and ample manhood savoring it for a moment; then I continued, "But I have ways, and those ways will not be aborted for one person. I don't give second chances. So *off with the head*," I laughed; then he began to beg and plead like any man would when threatened with the loss of their family jewels. There are a few men walking around with flaps like real live Mattel Ken dolls because of me. I'm sure they aren't talking about their situation because what man is going to reveal that type of information? Yes, some have killed themselves, but most just live on in shame and pain-filled flashbacks of what used to be. A memory of their last ejaculation did keep some alive.

The doctor came in and with the assistance of my men, wheeled him into the room that would forever change his life. It didn't take long, for the sounds of his pain could be heard throughout the compound. I had speakers in every area so I could make announcements and play warning sounds such as this one, reinforcing fear in the hearts of the ones that have pled loyalty and those with envious eyes. There is always someone waiting in the wings for your demise or a slipup, even the ones you trust.

Too many have come up against me and tried to take me and my organization down, but I won't be stopped. I had just about every illegal entity and activity on lock. Yes, there was a gay man on top, and that's how I intended it to stay. I would fight until the end. Nothing was off-limits to me or my crew. Baltimore was in for a rude awakening. We were taking dicks, and the city with it.

Chapter 2

Leroy

Pumped

"These dick chasers are fucking everywhere." I banged on my steering wheel as I pulled in the gas station. A car full of them was right at the pump in front of me. Music was blasting in the car, and they were gyrating and shaking their bodies. It made my stomach twitch. Other people around found it amusing, but I didn't. It was downright disgusting to me. Nobody wanted to see that shit.

I blew my horn, alerting them to my presence. They paused and looked at me, and then burst out into laughter. They commenced to continue their show and paid me no mind. I was seething on the inside.

I unbuckled my seat belt and went to unlock the car door when my wife reached over and touched me on the arm.

I turned and looked at her.

"Roy, what is up with you and gay people? They're not doing anything to you. Let them live," she said with pleading eyes.

"What the fuck you mean let them live?" I spat back at her. "This shit is just disrespectful. I don't want my son growing up seeing this shit. Shit is wrong as fuck."

"Roy, all of that tension and anger is not good for our son either. What about *that?*" She looked at me like she just checked me.

"Who the fuck side are you on?" I looked at her like she was crazy.

"*Side?* There are *no* sides, Roy. They just like you and me. Human."

"That shit ain't human or natural. That shit is nasty. They not real with all that shit going on. Real men don't act like that. Real men carry themselves with some fucking dignity and go hard for their family. Like I do and shit."

I unlocked the door and got out of the car and proceeded to do what I was about to do before she interrupted me.

"Roy, don't do nothing stupid," she warned me as I walked toward the Texaco payment station. One of *them* was in line waiting to pay. He looked me up and down as I walked up behind him.

"What the fuck are you looking at?" I barked at him.

He looked me up and down again, and then turned back around in line. His punk ass must have known better. He moved up to the counter and paid for his gas. As he left, he mugged me, and I mugged him right back. The look on my wife's face as she watched me watch him walk over to his car pleaded with me not to take it any further. Then I looked at my son in the backseat and cooled it down for him. He was my champ and my prince. I didn't want him to see me acting out over a faggot. I was going to get even later.

The only reason I was even at this gas station pumping my own gas was because my wife wanted to feel like a "real family" and not the great drug king's family that I was on my way to becoming. She wanted to go out on a "family outing" and not have one of my drivers with me. She didn't know that I always had someone on watch. She just couldn't see it. I had things on and popping, and my life was moving in the best direction possible.

The streets of Baltimore have always been my way of living since I could remember. I didn't have a sob story or a victim mentality. I just took shit as it came my way. I didn't punk out. When things got tough, I got tougher. I rolled with the punches. Life was not for no losers and wimps. I have taken lives and some more shit. I was in for the long haul. I looked at my family, and that shit drove me to let nothing stop me.

There was one problem that was keeping me from a full-fledged takeover of Baltimore City. These mutha-fuckin' faggots got some good shit going on, and it's dipping into my finances. I wasn't strapped for cash, but I knew that I was supposed to be making more money than I was bringing in. In fact, I was feeling the squeeze in several areas where I was normally bringing in big bucks. I did the normal shit like other drug lords do. I threatened a few of my lieutenants and even killed one or two that I presumed was skimming. I knew my men feared me, but they weren't my problem. My problem was with the addicts. They had a new drug of choice that was getting the best of my supplies. These days and ages, crack had taken a backseat to the real drug market. This new drug was something called Drank. It hit the city like crack in the eighties. This new generation is getting high any way they can. The thing is, nobody can track this guy that is at the top of this new Gay Mafia. I know a few police are watching me, but they can't get me on anything. But this guy is virtually invisible. I have a few police on the inside, and they are clueless as well. They have tried to get a picture of him, but he is elusive and cunning. Which lets me know that the money he's making is what *I* should be making. My main objective in life now is to find something better than what this guy is selling or get his spot and take his shit from him. I'm praying for the latter. There is nothing like taking what is rightfully yours. Real men should be running this city, not these he-shes.

Chapter 3

Monica

The Deep End

We were supposed to be having a nice outing with just us as a family, and I couldn't even enjoy it because of the hatred that was brewing inside of my husband. Being the wife of a very powerful drug dealer and even a legitimate business owner was not a problem for me. I grew up in various parts of Baltimore, but mostly the very dangerous parts. I've seen killings, robberies, and drug activities extensively in my lifetime. I was now as close to immune as one could get to it. My husband was very passionate about his family, and he does what it takes to keep us comfortable and happy. But as of late, he has been going off the deep end. He was awake most of night, meeting with his men at strange hours, and had just plain erratic behavior. I could deal with all of that if he didn't start pacing the house and talking to himself. Plus, he has guns in almost every room of the house. He didn't even care if my son saw them or not. He was starting to scare the shit out of me. When my eighteen-year-old son came up to me and told me about the conversations that his father was having with him, that's when I truly became fearful. I couldn't get the thoughts out of my mind.

"Ma, Dad said I could kill a guy if he comes on to me."
He looked up to me. I was bringing him his breakfast at the kitchen table.

"What!" I looked at him like he had lost his mind. "Your father didn't say that to you," I laughed, trying to make light of the situation. I didn't want my son to see that what he just said had rocked me to the core. Leroy was slowly losing his mind.

"No joke, Ma." He looked at me intensely. "He said all them faggots need to die a slow, painful death. When I was playing my Halo games, he was telling me how to shoot them in the head like I was doing while I was playing the game. He said just like those cops are killing us, we should be doing the same thing to them punks."

"Corey, your father was probably drunk or playing with you when he was saying those things. Don't take him serious." I looked him in the eyes to let him know that I was serious.

"He looked serious to me." The stony expression on his face matched that of his father's on the average day, so I knew that he wasn't joking. I joined him with my breakfast. We ate in silence. After about fifteen minutes, he got up from the table, put his empty plate in the sink, and walked off.

I shook my head because I didn't know what else my husband would do or tell my son. Shit, I don't know what the hell he was going to do to anyone. He was like a walking time bomb.

"Babe, look at that sun go down. Isn't that just beautiful?" I rested on my husband's chest as we coasted out on the Chesapeake. We were on a boat that I had my husband buy us so we could get away. We were from some of the grimiest parts of Baltimore, but that didn't mean that we didn't like the finer things in life. This boat cost us a pretty penny, but it was well worth it. Besides, now, we have plenty more money than we did when he first started hustling.

"Yeah, it's a'ight." He twisted up his face a little. I could only assume that he didn't want to be here because his focus went back to his phone after a few seconds; then he took a phone call which I was sure was business. He wanted to be somewhere planning this big takeover. His phone was in his hand the whole time, and I wanted to be where that phone was right now. In his hands. This was not a pleasure trip for me at all.

If I was the insecure type, I would be worried that he was sneaking around on me, but he's smarter than that. He knows that I am not one to play with. I wasn't with a drug dealer because I had prissy ways. I have five brothers, and they didn't play with dolls, and neither did I. I was a brawler for sure, but now I was a bit calmer than I was when I was in my twenties. My thirties have calmed me down a tad as well. I still would snatch a wig if I had to, but Roy knows that I would kill him, and the police would never find his body. My brothers work for him, so he knew better anyway.

"Roy, I thought we were supposed to be enjoying this time together without you focused on business." I gently caressed a few of the curly hairs on his chest. It was usually a cue for him to know that I wanted to be intimate.

"Monica, business never stops because I'm away. You know this." He got up aggressively and walked over to the edge of the boat. It pissed me off, but I let it slide because I didn't want to agitate the situation anymore. He was the man, and I was his woman. I knew my place. And this moment, I needed to let him be. He was good at his business, and I like the proceeds of said business.

I let him be and went below the deck to be with my son, who I know was playing his game. He was quiet, and that was one of the only things he did, as a boy like him would normally be jerking off or talking to girls on his phone.

Chapter 4

Corey

Just Normal

I was glad to be out here on the water with my parents. We felt like a normal family. Even though my dad has been bugging out for a minute now, we're still cool. He was just doing what he had to do for his family. I wasn't a normal kid in a normal family. I knew that my father was part of the reason that many of my friends didn't have some of their parents or other relatives due to the havoc that the drug market is wreaking on the city of Baltimore and plenty of the surrounding areas. We lived in the suburbs, but my father worked in the city, just like tons of blue-collar families. On paper, we lived in the city, but we resided out here in Westminster, Maryland. It was quiet as hell out here, but it was cool to not have to deal with the city life directly. I went to a city school and enjoy my city friends but went home to the quiet life. I was an eighteen-year-old at the beginning of my last year of high school. I had some learning challenges as a kid that caused me to be held back a grade, but now, I was one of the smartest in my class. My beginning didn't define my end, and I'm glad about it.

Anyway, I wasn't like everybody else. Normal. That was a big word that I didn't understand. What is normal? I didn't know, but I knew that I wasn't in the world's category of normal.

I'm gay. I like giving and taking dick. I have wrestled with it for so long now. I fought the urges and tried to ignore the fact that I wasn't the least bit interested in girls. I think that my mother knows about it. Most mothers know about these types of things by some type of instinct or something. If she does, she doesn't talk about it or question me at all.

My father, on the other hand, has a huge problem with the whole "new" gay agenda. So, what do you do when your father is hell-bent on destroying gay life and all involved? What does his son do? He keeps that shit to himself like the fuck he has been doing. I'll deal with it when it comes to that. For now, I'm a girl whore. It's all about the ladies for me as far as it concerns anyone else.

I was down here playing on my game and texting to this hot little piece of ass that wants me to smash soon. He was a piece of straight trade that lived a few houses down from me. We've been texting for a minute now, and I was so ready to give him the best dick of his life. He wasn't my first piece of ass, but I wanted to know how he felt on the inside. I personally couldn't wait until he was sliding up and down on my manhood. As for now, I just have to wait until the time is right. Tonight would have been perfect, but we both had family obligations.

I heard my mother coming downstairs, so I hid my phone underneath my pillow and pretended like I was fully concentrating on the game I was playing.

"Hey, baby, what level you up to?" she asked as she plopped down beside me on the bed. She wasn't all that knowledgeable about the games I played, but it was fun watching her pretend as if she cared.

"The hard level." I laughed and continued to play the game that was just on pause a few seconds ago.

"You are such a smart-ass." She playfully pushed me. I loved my mom. She wasn't all mushy and emotional. She was quite tough. I loved that about her. She wasn't a man by a long shot, though. She was an absolute lady. "So who was the chick that you were down here texting before I got down here? And why is your phone under the pillow?"

"Ma, I wasn't texting anyone."

"Are you sure that's your final answer?" She looked at me with an expressionless face. I was stalling. I wasn't going to give in. My father taught me that.

"Yep." I continued to look ahead at the game on the television screen.

"So that flashing light underneath that pillow is what?" I heard her say while mentally kicking myself. I was caught. I gave in, paused my game once again, reached under the pillow, and pulled out my phone. That had a text message notification blinking a green light that she saw against the white of the pillow. I didn't push it far enough under the pillow. I should remind myself to turn that shit off as soon as I get a chance.

I looked at my phone and saw that it was a message from Greg. I had his name under a female name like I did with all the other guys that I was trying to get with. I was a good-looking chocolate brother with defining features that men and women loved. I came from good stock, as they say.

"Who the hell is Michelle and when are we going to meet her?" My mother leaned over and looked at the screen of my phone, and then leaned back. I could feel her looking at me and waiting for answer.

"When the time is right, you and Dad will get to meet Michelle. It's not rock solid yet, so I'm not going to waste her and y'all's time with something that probably won't work out. Feel me?" I looked at her in the eyes with a serious look on my face. I was being genuine now. I did want them to meet my mate when the time was right and the person was right. I was waiting just as much as they were to meet the one.

"Corey, don't be out here fucking these skanky broads without any protection. Most young girls are up to no good these days, and they are always trying to trap the next guy that is about something."

"You don't have to worry about that. I strap up every time."

"So your ass is fucking. I knew you were. I just needed confirmation, and you just gave it to me." She looked at me and shook her head. It didn't look like a totally disagreeing shake but more of a concerned one. "My baby is all grown up. What am I going to do with you?"

"I don't know, but could you leave me alone so I can get my mack on in private?" I laughed.

"Damn, both my men are acting funny. Let's see how this plays out when you guys want something to eat," she laughed as she got up from beside me.

I laughed as well, and then breathed a sigh of relief, knowing that she was now gone up on the deck. I was so glad that she didn't grab my phone and scroll up because she would have seen an ass and dick shot that "Michelle" just sent me. That would have been a hard thing to explain, and the gig would have been up.

Chapter 5

Clayton

APB

Baltimore used to be "The City that Reads." Now, it's "The City that Breeds" . . . crime, that is. I've been a cop for a long time now, and the crime in the city has taken a turn for the worse. "Just say no" is out the window and people are getting high off anything. The age group has changed as well. I've never arrested or seen so many strung out kids in all my life. Now, we have a new crime wave going on by this Gay Mafia that is setting this city ablaze. They are flooding the streets with this new "Drank" drug. It's a mixture of a controlled cough syrup called promethazine mixed with soda or something close to it. It didn't take much to get high off it. I'm learning that with a sip or two, you can coast on a high for an hour or two. The adverse effects were devastating, however. The heart is its target, and it's killing many people . . . or leaving them in a serious, irreversible condition.

I was sitting at my desk waiting for a parent to come to my office to give me some details on the case I was looking over now. Their daughter was now on a respirator, among other machines, keeping her "alive." I had the task of going to the hospital a few days ago to look at her, and it blew my mind. I don't have any children, but the presence of so many machines and tubes and things running in and out of this child's body was heartbreaking. As I stood in the room and took all of it in, it saddened me to see this, and it also made me wonder what could drive a child to do something like this to herself. Was it peer pressure, family issues, or experimentation? None of the answers could bring this young adolescent back to her healthy state before the drug she had consumed.

"This is so heartbreaking," I heard a voice say from behind me. I turned to see a black man with a white jacket on. I assumed he was the resident doctor and care-giver for this patient. "I've had so many patients come in here because of this new drug, yet I am still disheartened every time a new one shows up. It's an epidemic. One we never saw coming." He shook his head. One could see that he was sincere in what he said. He walked over to the young girl's bed and gently ran his hand up and down one of her hands. There was no response from her. Never would be again.

"Yes, you are so right," I agreed. "This cannot be allowed to go on."

"What can be done?" he probed. "This is happening right in front of us, and no one knows where it's coming from or who is flooding the streets with this new killer."

"There is always someone at the top. Always someone to answer for the lives lost. No one can stay hidden forever. This person will slip up, and there will be someone there to catch them. Always." I felt the conviction in my heart as I spoke these words. How can someone mercilessly peddle this drug in the streets among the other drugs that continue to plague the world? This person had to be caught and brought to justice.

"I sure hope that somebody does something soon. This is just cruel." He shook his head. I couldn't help but notice that this doctor was very good looking. I almost got lost in the gaze of his eyes.

"I'll do my best. By the way, my name is Detective Stewart. I'm lead detective on these cases." I reached out to shake his hand. He didn't hesitate to do the same.

"I'm Dr. Anthony Moore. I'm the attending physician for this ward and a specialist dealing with substance abuse and the trauma that results from the use, though treating patients this young is new and heartbreaking for me. I'm doing my best to cope and leave my personal feelings out of this."

"Yes, I can only imagine." I nodded my head. "I too have the same sentiments you have."

As we stood in the middle of the room talking, two people made their way into the room. Their faces were flushed with tears, and their shoulders were slumped. Sorrow was a part of their life right now. I could only imagine their thoughts since I was without a child.

"Mr. and Mrs. Rogers, this is Detective Stewart. He's going to find the person that is responsible for your daughter's present state," Doctor Moore said as he looked at them, and then at me.

The lady, who looked to be in her early thirties, was overcome with grief. She sobbed and fell into the arms of the man that she was with.

"I hope you find him before I do, because when I do, he won't suffer like my baby girl is doing right now." The man spoke gruffly as he consoled the mother.

"I will do my best." I spoke with confidence.

"Do better," he scowled, and then a few curse words came afterward. He pulled his wife closer and then focused their attention back on their child. I felt some type of way about his tone and harsh words but dismissed it. I knew that he was running on pure adrenaline and pain right now. Most would, given the current situation.

"Doctor, I will keep in touch, and I hope you do the same." I reached in my pocket and handed him one of my cards. I secretly hoped that he would call me. More about getting to know him than the case. Mixing business and pleasure was something that shouldn't be done, but I knew I could keep the two separated. I'm a great multitasker, and this wouldn't be hard to do.

"I will do so," he said as he took the card. He looked interested. Or maybe that was my own hope.

I exited the room and the hospital. As I drove back to the precinct, I thought about how much I have let go to get to where I was in my career. I rarely got a chance to date with the workload that I had, and the ones that I did have were only one-night stands to do what I was tired of letting my hand do. I had hopes about this case and ones about the doctor, as well. Companionship would be nice, especially with one that shares the same passion for justice and people as I do.

Chapter 6

Avery

In Plain Sight

I moved with a smile. I was a nice guy. That is what they saw. My deep, smooth, baritone voice was a great deceiver to many. The world's view of the gay man was still archaic and patchy. They thought they had a lock on us, but they weren't even close. We were all around them. The least likely, as they say.

I was walking among the people in one of Baltimore's breeding grounds and hoarding house of all kinds of activities. Lexington Market is a staple for Baltimore. Known for its food and other delicacies, this is where it's at. The meeting place for the depressed, hungry, horny, hungover, and lowlifes of the city. Any kind of drug could be found here without even looking hard. Getting high or low was just a nod away. I had a few vendors in here selling as well. You could order a sandwich, chicken, or a hot dog, and get a hit of Drank with at least ten vendors in here. This is where a good deal of my money came from. I had other drugs on deck, but Drank was my moneymaker for sure. I looked around as I walked, and some of my workers were doing their thing. They didn't even know me. They were at the bottom of the ladder. Only a few people knew who I was or what I looked like.

I came in here to get high myself. I was getting high off the downfall of the city. Every bent over person was pumping me with power. This place was already down before I got here. All they needed was another shove to the ground by "The Man." It wasn't the government that people had to worry about. It was me, a gay man. A quiet force to be reckoned with. There was a very well-known ransom on my head. They just didn't know where to look. I didn't dress the part, but I was very gay and very rich. In plain sight is where your worst enemy is at most of the time. I stood among them, complained with them, slummed with them, or at least that is what it looked like to them. But like a vampire, I vanished without a trace, disappearing into the open shadows of the night until it was time to come out and check on my business.

"Hey, Mr. Clarence, you want the regular today?" the clerk asked as I stepped up in the line I was in and leaned on the counter a bit. They smiled hard when I came. I was a regular. They loved regulars, and so did I. It's why their business thrived and mine as well. We worked hand in hand, and they didn't even know it. My products were the reason they were still in business. An addict was almost always hungry down here.

"Yeah, give me the usual." I flashed my smile. It didn't take long for them get my order together and for me to make my way to the mezzanine level of the building where I could survey the land like any other king. It was the sit-down area for all the ones that could brave the madness all around. The addicts sat in groups, and a few nodded off during their conversations. It was a sad sight to many, but one I lived to see. The decay of the city was rampant. City politicians scrambled to get a grip on it, but it was like a wild spreading fungus. What could you do with the invisible? Not a thing. I was free to reign.

"Hey, yo, where've you been?" a "friend" said as he approached the table I was sitting at devouring my food. This place did serve up a great meal. He was a vagrant and frequented this place for his next come up or scam. I indulged him most of the time because he kept me in the loop per se. I had informants, but there was nothing like getting it from the mouth of an addict. It was unadulterated.

"Hey, wassup, partna?" I rose from my seat, gripped his hand in a tight clasp, and we embraced in a nonthreatening, masculine hug. To the normal eye, it was two homeboys coming together to chat a little like most men did in the world of masculinity.

I sat back down in my seat; then he sat down across from me. I waited until I thought he was comfortable; then I answered his question. "Man, I've been chilling and shit. My old lady bugging the hell out of me to get a job, and my fucking kids tearing shit up. You know, the usual." I laughed, and so did he.

"I hear that, dude." He nodded his head. "Same shit over here. Baby momma's on my back about finances and shit. I'm bugging like crazy. Getting ready to crank up this loud I got in my pocket and head on over to this shorty house to try to put this rib back in her chest through her pussy. I need to release me some stress through a good nut. Ain't nothing like breaking a bitch back, and then smoking me a thick one, or vice versa. Those problems will be there when my high goes down."

We both laughed, but I was laughing at him and not with him. He was just like the rest of my financiers; hooked on phonics and stuck on stupid.

"That is some real truth right there, partna." I nodded my head. "I'm about to score me some shit and head on back home myself." I began to wrap up my leftover food and stood up.

"It's been real, homie," I said as I gave him dap with a balled-up fist. "It's time to be getting back in. This bitch is blowing up my phone like crazy. She just praying for me to put my hands on her when I get there. It's like she be asking for it, yo."

"Man, you ain't neva lied. Sometimes you have to Ike Turner these hoes to keep them quiet." We laughed together again.

"Next time, partna," I said as I nodded my head and moved back down the stairs and out into the streets that I be taking over block by block.

Chapter 7

Leroy

Give It Up

I sat on the balcony of the luxury town house that we lived in, out in the surrounding suburbs of Baltimore County. I was a city man all day, but this life that I lived because of the city life and the streets, I enjoyed. It felt like it was slipping away from me, though, the grasp that I once had on the city. I was almost there, and then this ghost muthafucker came in and began syphoning off the market I was popular in. I had coke, crack, pills, and heroin on lock, but this new drug was easier to get, and distribution was faster, and overall, it was new. It reached a new market as well, the teen market. So now the adult and the teens were getting high off this syrup, and it was widespread.

"This shit is driving me nuts," I said as I tapped the gun I had in my hand against my head. I was thinking of ways to get on top of this situation. This ghost guy and his constituents were very loyal. I have even kidnapped a few of his workers. I've tortured them and all. They were some tough little dick takers.

I snatched a few of his workers from a few areas that they were known to frequent. All you had to do to find the seller is follow or entice the addict. It seemed like it would be easy as pie. I've done it before with regular dealers and almost always got what I wanted but not with these ones.

I looked out into the room where we had three of the Ghost's workers tied up like Kunta Kinte, from the ceiling. Three of my lieutenants were also in the room. I was optimistic that I was going to be getting some good information today that would lead to the overhaul of this dude's growing empire. These guys that he had working for him weren't your typical gay dudes as it comes to looks, though. They were tough, and one even looked tougher than one of my men. That didn't deter me, though. I was on a mission of control and power.

We had all types of torture equipment in the room to get the information that I needed. Chains, electric prodder sticks, acid, and one lethal tactic. My logic was three was better than one. Having three in the room and having them watch each other get tortured would bring one to eventually give up the goods.

We started with the first one, upon whom we used electrocution as a tool to get him to talk.

"Where you get your shit from?" I asked him as one of my men poked him with an electric prodder. His body twitched and lurched a bit, but no words came out of his mouth. I motioned for him to be jabbed again with the prodders but longer this time. Same results, but he did cry out a little. The fear on the face of the other two as their partner was being tortured gave me pleasure. Partly because I was envisioning the dude at the gas station from the other day.

I had him jabbed until he passed out. It was expected, and I knew that it was just to show the other two that I was serious and about business. It was on to the next one.

With this one, we pulled out the acid-filled syringes. This was one that I knew would give me the results that I needed. Pain was no one's friend, and this surely would deliver. We started by squeezing out a small drop to the back of the second victim. He twitched and groaned, but that was it.

"You gonna talk or what? I know this shit hurts. I know unlike a real man that you can't take this too much longer. Just give me the information I want, and this is the end of it." It was all a lie, of course. They weren't leaving here the same way they came, for sure.

He shook his head no. It infuriated me.

"Put some all over his head," I instructed but held my hand up for my man to pause.

"You gonna talk, or I'm going to let him do what I just said?" I was up in his face as I spoke. They all had rags tightly wrapped around their mouths, but his eyes said fuck you; then he lowered his head as if to say, "go ahead and do it." I had to admit that there was heart in that silent statement. It almost made me respect him.

"Go ahead and give it to him," I instructed my man. The thrashing and gritting groans from the guy probably would have been louder if his mouth wasn't covered. He was in deep pain. Tears flowed freely from his eyes.

"Talk, muthafucka," I bellowed, and then punched him in the gut as if the pain that he was already in wasn't enough. I didn't care. I wanted answers. By this time, the first guy was back to consciousness and looking like he was spent.

Neither guy said anything. They looked at the wall in front of them with stony faces. This was pissing me off. They were supposed to have given in by now. These faggots were loyal as fuck.

"I guess it's your turn now," I said as I walked up to the last guy. The last guy was the well-built one, and the one

my men said was hard to take down. The last torture I had up my sleeve I was sure was going to get me some results.

"I need you to pay very close attention to what is about to happen in the next few seconds. You need to know that this is not a game. I need names, locations, suppliers. Any information you can give me. Are you willing to talk?" I talked to him directly in his ear. I wanted him to feel the seriousness, my hot breath, and every syllable I spoke.

He ignored me just like the rest.

"Let's see how much you ignore me after this." I motioned one of the men to come over to me with a silver serving tray that had some cloth covering my last tactic. I walked over to the first guy and pulled off the cloth to the tray while my men held it.

"You know what that is?" I asked, knowing that he couldn't answer me. "This here is a death sentence in a syringe. No, this is not the HIV virus. This is full-blown AIDS. It's ready to enter your veins and body and wreak havoc until you are dead. I'm sure you faggots have seen what this can do to a person and the pain that it causes. I'm also sure that you don't want to die this way. Not for a guy that doesn't give a rat's ass about you. He doesn't care. I know you are not willing to die for him." I spoke so all of them could hear me.

I let that marinate for a minute. I wasn't a total tyrant. I let three minutes go by to let it sink in.

"Anybody ready to talk? Just nod your head and all of this will be over." I tried to sound as convincing as I possibly could, though I was lying.

No one said a thing.

"Inject the first one," I told my men. The first one took the shot without even blinking. I looked at the other two to see if they had any reactions. None. I moved on to the second one.

"Speak or this is it for you. No more time. Give me the answers I want." He said nothing. His eyes were fixed on the wall as if he wasn't even there.

"Inject him." I waved my hand and walked over to the last one.

"You've seen the results of not giving up answers. The other two don't have a chance at a normal life as of now, but you do. All I need is answers." I spoke in a tone different from the other two. It was a patient and calm voice. I was hoping that he would hear the quietness in my voice, and it would reach him somehow. It was my stab at manipulation since these guys were used to being weak and quiet.

I continued, *"I know you want to give me the answers. Think about your family. You don't want to put them through this. This is not like you all. You all are always considerate and nice. This tough role you are putting on is not you. Just give me the answers and I swear you will leave here the way you came."*

I backed up off him and let him think about it for five minutes. I was being nice. A rare trait, these days, for me.

"Talk." My patience was gone. I was in his face once again. Not one response. The embarrassment of the situation infuriated me even more. I felt like one of them right now: a weak, muthafuckin' faggot.

"Stick him and unload them all back to where you found them." Those were the last words I said before I left where we were located.

That was two days ago, and here I am now, up all night long trying to come up with something else to do to get what I wanted. I will stop at nothing to get what I want.

I want it all.

Chapter 8

Monica

Restless

I awoke to an empty bed once again. It was something I was used to when I knew that my husband was out in the streets. I felt safe knowing that is where he was at times. The streets were safe for the ones that were raised in them. At least, that's what helps me sleep easier at night. Now the bed was empty because he was losing his mind with this "gay" problem. We had money. Plenty of it. But that wasn't enough for him. He wanted it all: money, power, and control. I've seen this on many television shows, but it was playing out in my life. It was getting old fast. I liked when my husband was in control and looked the part. He said things, gave orders, and men followed. It was all in line. But now he was just different. It was making me crazy seeing him go crazy. It was like one of those smart Asian kids failing a test, and then committing suicide, or a stock broker when the stock market fails, but at a much slower pace. Leroy wasn't eating the same. His attention span with me and our son had diminished greatly.

I pulled the covers off me, grabbed my Chanel house-coat, and exited my sleeping chamber to walk around the house to see where he was or if he was in the house. It didn't take me long to find him out on the balcony. He was laid out on some of our patio furniture with some liquor on one side of him and a gun on the other side of him. I looked through the glass door at him for a bit. Pity filled my stomach and my mind. I slowly opened the door to the patio/balcony and walked the short distance to where he was. His hands and arms were laid out beside him like he had passed out from exhaustion. As I got to him, I stood in front of him and looked at him. His head was slumped over, and droplets of drool ran down the side of his face. I shook my head and then walked over to his side. I crouched down and gently shook him.

"Roy, baby," I softly spoke but got no response. I shook him harder, and then called out his name louder than before.

"Roy."

With surprise and force, he lurched forward and threw his hands around my neck, knocking me to the ground, and then pinning me underneath him. It happened so fast that it knocked the wind out of me, so much so that I couldn't attempt to call out to him to get him off me.

Then suddenly, he was off me. I looked up and saw my son standing there. Leroy was on the ground a few feet from me.

"Dad, what the hell are you doing?" He looked at his father as if he was going to kill him.

I couldn't say anything because I was trying to get my breath back under control. But I did put my hand up to motion to my son to stop.

"Damn, baby," Leroy said as he rubbed his face and crawled over to where I was. "I'm sorry. I don't know what came over me. I was having this wild-ass dream; then you woke me up and . . ." He didn't finish. He just got up and walked past my son and into the house.

"Ma, you okay?" Corey asked as he reached down to pick me up. It was a Saturday, and he's usually still asleep right now, but I remembered as he helped me over to one of the chairs that it was basketball practice day, so he was up getting ready to leave soon. I almost never went out with him to his sporting events because his father usually did. His schooling was usually where I was most active. It was a great balance in the household . . . until now. This was his first try at basketball, and he was nervous. He didn't say it, but I felt it.

My son was very active in sports, and he played for many teams in his life. This was an outside-of-school team. It was a recreational team in Baltimore City. He said it was the hood boys that played the best. I had to agree. As a young girl in the hood, basketball and football were hood sports or the ones that the youngest men gravitated toward. I watched many games being played with the hood boys as a young girl. Basketballs, tight bodies, basketball shorts, and drug dealers were the summers I remember, and now my son wants to be in the city life. My husband and I wanted the best for our son, even though we didn't go about it legally; but we still wanted better for him.

Moving him from the city to the country was a move my husband said would be good for all of us. Trying to keep work and home separate was his goal. It was working . . . until now. Corey was an only child, and we were very protective of him. He knew his father's mode of business, but Leroy kept him as far away from that life as possible. He didn't want him to fall into the street life. He didn't want him to be a punk either, just a better version of him. A legal him. I think that was a part of Leroy's drive to get to the top, as he says it.

I peeked out of the upstairs window to see my husband's car gone. I don't know if he got dressed or not because I was in the bathroom prepping to leave myself. Leroy's erratic behavior was driving me crazy right now.

"Ma! Where Daddy go?" my son came into my bedroom and asked just as I was coming out of the bathroom. He had a look of disappointment on his face.

"He said he would be right back and asked me to go with you to practice today," I lied. I didn't want to add to the tension already between him and his father. I could see that his father's behavior was getting to him as well. Leroy was staying out later and communicating less. It seemed like we were growing apart.

"You going with me?" He looked at me like I was an alien.

"Uh, yeah." I laughed a little to lighten up the heaviness of this morning's strange activities.

"Ma, you know nothing about basketball. Why are you really going?" He had a silly smirk on his face. It lightened the moment for me as well. He was the spitting image of his father with a dash of me thrown in.

"So, I want to see what all the hype's about. I heard your father say you had a nice crossover, and I wanted to see if that was true."

"I bet," he smiled. "Just don't be embarrassing me and all of that. Stay incognegro." He laughed, and I couldn't help but laugh with him. He was such a great kid. With good grades, cool friends, and an outgoing attitude, my son was coming out to be a well-rounded young man. I was a proud mama.

It didn't take us long to finish getting ready and heading out into the streets for some fun in the sun.

Chapter 9

Corey

Promises

I was in the passenger seat of my mother's car wondering what just happened. I have never seen my father look like that before. He looked like one of the junkies that he made our living off of. I was so close to beating his ass that I could taste it. I didn't like that feeling. I had mad respect for my father. He was what I wanted to be when I got on my own. He was a hard-core, no-nonsense man that loved his family and taking care of business. He was passionate. That's what made me hold off on dusting him off good. He was almost a dude in the street to me. My mother's voice also saved him too. I was my father's size and build, though I was a little bit more muscular than he was. He would have caught a good ass whipping. Believe that.

"Ma, has Dad ever been like this before?" I inquired.

"Like what?" she asked. She knew what I meant. As of late, she has been downplaying most of his strange behavior. He wasn't acting normal, and she knew it. I didn't like being played for a dummy by anyone, even my mother.

"Ma, if I didn't get there when I did, you might be at the hospital or dead right now. *That's* what I'm talking about." I had a slight tone that was borderline disrespectful. She was taking up for him. It was her husband and my father. I get that, but don't push that shit under the rug like it didn't happen or something. That not cool.

"Who the hell are you basing on?" She quickly glanced at me with a look that put fear back in my heart. "I only need one hand to drive this car and the other one to break your jaw. Adjust . . . your . . . tone!"

There was immediate silence on my end for the next minute.

"Ma, all I'm saying is keep your eyes open. I love you, and I don't want to lose you."

"Corey, your father is not going to kill me or hurt me. He's just going through something right now, and we need to bear with him until it passes." We were at a red light, and she looked at me with tears threatening to fall. She looked like she wanted to break down. My mom was a strong woman, but you can't deny that she had some doubt floating around in her head. Any person would if their spouse was acting a fool like my father was.

"Okay, Ma, I'm going to ride with you on this one, but if it happens again, believe me, I *will* handle my business. Father or no father."

We rode in silence as we pulled up to the gymnasium. I still had the drama from home on my brain as I walked through the door, and that's what was going to drive me to do my best.

Chapter 10

Clayton

Man of the House

From a distance, I sat in my car and watched the activities called crimes being acted out in daring disregard for the law. There was a war going on between two sets of thugs: the gays and the straight.

So, who do you take down, or do you try to take down all of them? I'm a gay man, and you would think that I would automatically side with the gay thugs, right? No. They are both in the wrong. I'm trying to get up in the ranks, and there are no winners and losers. With drugs on the streets, there are only losers, even the ones that get to profit from it all. One day, they will end up in jail or dead. It's just a matter of time. But I couldn't wait for time. Time was too damn slow for me. I need to catch someone slipping. That's just it. No one wanted to be a rat these days. There was always a paid informant or druggie that was willing to snitch for their next hit or freedom. But no one was giving up any information. With business, the way it was for these hood-rich folk, they would be going for a long time before someone gave in and started snitching, as they say.

I had an idea, and I only hoped that it would work. But that was for later. Right now, I had the doctor I met a few days ago on the brain. I wanted to get some ass, and it has been a minute. I know that I should be focused on the matters at hand, but I was a human being. I had urges and needs. My hand wasn't good enough. Let's just say if my hand could get pregnant, I would have a small nation on my hands by now.

I wanted to feel the warm walls inside of a tight, strong, anal cavity. I was getting hard just thinking about it. I could feel him already sliding up and down on my rock-hard penis until I exploded inside of him. The sheer joy it would be to give the best that I had. There were so many times that I wanted to go to the meat rack district and pull me a trick, but that would be taking a chance. A chance that I didn't want to take. Too many people were being exposed right now, and I didn't, and wouldn't, have that on my record. I loved having a clean slate, and that's the way that I wanted to keep it. No one on the force even knew that I was gay. It was still considered a weakness to a great percentage of the world in this day and time.

I was tired of this scene as of right now, and I decided to go and hook up with Anthony. We've been texting on and off for a few days now, and he finally invited me out for a spur-of-the-moment bite to eat. I was bubbling with excitement, and I was hoping that it leads to me losing some weight in my family jewels.

"This is a really nice place," I said as I sat across the table from Anthony. He was glowing tonight, or maybe it was the fact that I hadn't had any real ass in a minute. Things can get distorted in our minds and the way we see them when we're desperate. I didn't care, though. I was just glad to hopefully be in the beginning stages of a possible relationship. I hoped it would be a long-term one as well.

"Yes, this is one of my favorite spots to eat out and just to enjoy myself. I love delicate and fancy places." He smiled.

"I love someone with some good taste. It speaks volumes about their life and choices." I was trying my best not to sound like an idiot and keep the focus on him. I didn't want our first date to be all about me. No one likes that, at least not the people I tend to accompany myself with.

"My life wasn't always easy, and getting to where I am right now was not easy. It took time and sacrifice to get the finer things in life. I'm enjoying myself, and now, all I need is someone to share it with. It gets lonely at the top." He lowered his eyes a little and then lifted them back up and at me. It was nice to know that someone was on my wave length and could relate to me. It was a plus in my book. A turn-on too. Maybe anything he said was a turn-on to me. I was horny, but I didn't want to play my hand and mess things up.

"I can totally relate to that. Finding a good mate that can fulfill all of your needs and understand you is such a good thing, and it's missing from relationships these days," I spoke hoping that I was racking up some points to get me in that bed of his. I could almost hear his cries of pleasure as I worked my manhood in and out of him.

"Yes, and sex. I love a guy that can work it good. I'm a classy guy, but I love a man that can work me over and intimidate me in the bedroom. I have a superior mind and love to be dominated in the bedroom." He smiled and then blushed. He didn't know I wanted to take his ass in the bathroom and break his ass off something good right now. But since we both were upstanding citizens, we could carry on like that in public.

"Yes, that's high on my list as well. I'm all about being dominant and territorial too. What's mine is mine. I will be the man of the house in my house." I spoke confidently. I believed it wholeheartedly.

"Sounds like we're in agreement on many things." Anthony nodded his head.

"Yes, it indeed does sound like it."

"So where do we go from here?" Anthony asked.

"Let's take it slow and see where things lead us." I couldn't believe I just said that, knowing my dick was on fire for his ass. I wanted to fuck like never before, but I didn't want to come on too strong. Sex on the first date was still taboo in my book, even with my strong urges going on.

"Well, sir, you take the lead, and I will follow. I will play my part if you play yours."

"Agreed." I smiled. My ego was on cloud nine. It was the only thing that made me back off sex for the night. I guess me and my hand would be one once again tonight. But that wouldn't last too long. I'm sure of it.

Chapter 11

Avery

Chameleon

Having facelessness had very numerous perks, including being whatever you wanted to be. Right now, I was a basketball coach for inner-city kids. It was a pleasure for me because I wasn't a totally evil person. I loved kids, and I loved to help them be all they could be. It wasn't my first year doing this, and they were a fresh batch of kids ready to be pushed to the limits.

I watched as each one of them entered the gymnasium with or without their parents. This was a city organization that I have been a part of for quite some time. I loved basketball as a kid, but I was gay, and you couldn't be gay and play basketball. Another guy on the team decided to come out of the closet, and things didn't end good for him. They taunted him to no end. They called him names and stripped him naked once and made him walk home with a sign that said he was a "dick lover." I ditched it, and who I am today was forged out of that void.

About twenty young men and a few parents filled the wooden bleachers that stood on one side of the court. I looked at all of them for a few seconds. They were all silent waiting for me to speak. The anticipation on the faces of the young men and the parents was feeding me. I loved the attention and the control I could have over people, and right now was no different than any other situation.

"Welcome to my court. You young men come here to be trained and to sharpen your skills in the area of basketball. You want to be the next LeBron James. Well, fuck LeBron James. Aspire to be like him. No, be *better* than him. From this day on, this will be training in basketball and life. You're not going to leave here better, but you will leave here the best. This will not be fun, and you will fucking hate me by the end of the day. Parents, you are dismissed. Get the fuck off my court and leave these bastards here for me to shape and mold."

They looked at me as if I had lost my mind. The shock was apparent on the faces of the adults the most. One of the boys started to laugh. I guess he thought I was joking.

"Parents, I said get the fuck off my court. Pick these pieces of shit up in approximately three hours. Be late and I will make you pay for it." There was an immediate silence in the room as the adults, mainly women, began to exit the building one by one.

No one challenged me, and the laughter was just a memory.

"Give me 100 laps *now*," I barked. Most of them jumped up with youthful enthusiasm, but one or two lagged behind.

"Last one to finish will do an extra twenty-five laps. Don't waste my time, sissies. I *will* make you pay for it." I love to make threats *and* follow up with them.

I sat at the top of the bleacher with a stopwatch in my hand, and I focused on the ones that stuck out the most. There were at least three that stuck out to me. Everyone had the possibility to be a leader. These three would be the ones that I fucked with the most. They will be hating me very quickly.

Two hours later they were finished running, tired, and most of all, looked at me with displeasure. I loved it.

I gave them two minutes to catch their breath.

"Line up shoulder to shoulder. Don't make me wait," I yelled as I stood in the middle of the gymnasium. They followed instructions to a tee.

I walked down the line and looked at each one of them in the eyes. Some waivered, some did not move or flinch. I walked away in silence. I'm sure they were wondering what I was doing. The minds of these young men were going crazy. I knew it and, again, I loved it.

"I'm going to walk up to you and tap you on the shoulder. When I do, drop and begin to do push-ups, and you won't stop until I tell you. The rest of you can take a seat in the bleachers." I did as I said, and, so did they. I loved when people followed instructions correctly. I loved teachable people.

Half an hour later, there was only two young men of the three that were still performing. They were moving slowly but still going. Neither one would give in. I walked over to the equipment room where I kept some weights and pulled off two twenty-pound weights and placed one on each of the boys, and they continued to do push-ups, small breaks in between. The other boys looked on in amazement. I wasn't impressed yet. I want one of them to win. Yes, I had a favorite already. He looked like he had something to prove. He reminded me a bit of myself.

Fifteen minutes later, my favorite pulled it off. His opponent wasn't a chump. He was a great runner-up.

"Everyone, line up again," I instructed. They moved in line as if they were army men, and I was the sergeant.

"You . . . step forward." My favorite stepped forward. He looked exhausted and worn but still wore a serious expression on his face. He was different.

"What's your name?"

"Corey," he answered with no emotion.

"Corey, turn around and look at the others, and then turn back to me.

"This is your team. You are their leader. You lose, they lose, I lose. I don't like losing. Don't lose." I punched him in the stomach as hard as I could. He folded and hit the floor right in front of me.

"That is what life is to all of us. This is the end of today's lesson. Get your asses outside and wait for your parents." I walked away.

Chapter 12

Leroy

A Hit

Money always brings out the scavengers and the low-lifes. And today, one of my lieutenants came across what is hopefully a gold mine. A lead in the right direction. I was on my way across town to meet this person with some information. I was high on adrenaline, weaving in and out of traffic trying to get to my destination in a hurry. I was not naïve about my state of mind. I *was* a little unstable. The craving and hunger for power and control can do that to you. I chalked it up to paying the cost to be the boss. I didn't care how I looked. I would deal with the consequences later.

My mind drifted to a few days before when I snapped on my wife, and my boy had to pull me off her. I was still a bit confused about that situation. I didn't apologize that day because my wife knows how I am, and that I would never intentionally hurt her. But the look on my son's face as he pulled me off her was one that I would never forget. He was ready to do what he had to do to protect his mother. I commend him for that, and I'm glad that he didn't back down, even from me, even though I would have had to show him that I was still king of the jungle. Yes, he had more muscle on him than I did, but muscle didn't amount to experience. I have tossed up a grown man twice his size with no problem. I would not hurt my son, but he *would* remember the day.

I'm sure he's wondering what I'm doing and why I hadn't been very attentive these last few days. It wasn't strange for them to see me busy trying to keep the empire and legacy going that I had built from the ground up. It was a part of the cost of being a boss. My family will be fine. This life is everything to me. My name is on this. My name still rang in the streets, and I intended on keeping it that way with everything in me.

I would make it up to them both with more than they could ever imagine. I swore on it.

I finally made it to one of my stash houses. I pulled around back. I saw a few of my men on the way through the block, so I knew that I was protected. I always had protection, even when it didn't look like it.

I rushed out of the car and into the building with haste and my blood pressure rising. I was smiling on the inside, but my face was as a stone statue. There was no room for weakness.

"Where he at?" I questioned my lieutenant.

"In here, Boss. Waiting for you." He was a guy close to my age who had been with me for a long time. People knew not to cross me, and the dead ones spoke for my reputation.

I opened the door and saw a man in a seat behind a table. He had on all black with dark sunglasses on. Two of my men had automatically followed me in the room. I loved the control that I had over people.

I sat down in front of him and said nothing for a few seconds.

"Take his glasses off. I want to look into the eyes of the one that sits in my presence."

They did as I instructed. The guy that sat before me was frail. It looked like he hadn't had a good night's sleep in weeks. He looked like he was on one of the many drugs that I flooded the streets of Baltimore with.

"I hear you have some information for me?"

"Ye-yes. I just want to get this over with and get the money promised me. I really need it."

"I bet." I looked at him suspiciously. "What for? What's the money for? Why do you want my money?"

"That's personal," he said, and then looked down. Like he had shame or something to hide. It piqued my interest. I knew that I was here for information on this ghost character, but I wanted to know what would make someone desperate enough to come snitch on someone else. All snitching is about personal gain.

"Don't fucking play with me. Spit that shit out!" I said, and then banged on the table. He jumped.

"Okay," he nodded his head, and then pushed his chair back and stood up. My men instantly drew their weapons. I put my hand up signaling them not to shoot.

He began to unbuckle his pants and then proceeded to take them off.

"What the fuck are you doing?" I said, causing him to pause.

"You said you wanted to see why I needed the money. I'm about to show you." He then continued to pull his pants down, and then his boxers.

"Bitch, I don't want to see your dick. I have one of my own," I snarled.

"You don't have to worry about that," he said as he pulled down his boxers to expose the area that was *supposed* to house his genitals.

My mouth hung open in sheer shock and disbelief. "What the fuck!" I got up out of my chair and turned toward my men. I instinctively cupped my dick and balls with thanksgiving.

"*He* did this to me. He said I crossed him, and this was my punishment. I acted like a pussy, and now I have one." He spoke with my back still turned to him. I had to say this ghost guy had some shit with him. I see why he had the following that he had. No one wanted to lose their fleshy manhood.

"Man, pull your shit up. I've seen enough." I was still turned with my back to him. I felt sorry for him.

"You wanted answers. Don't ask questions when you're not ready for the answers. I want the money to make me a man again."

I finally turned back around, and he was seated back in the chair with his head hung low once again.

"So what information do you have for me?"

"I know where one of his stash houses is."

"I see. Show me where it is, and I'll give you what you came here for."

His face lit up with a smile.

I signaled my men to get him in custody once again, and we all loaded up into two cars. He was in the front one with two of my men, and I was traveling behind them in a car with three more of my guys. I didn't know if this was a setup or what, but I didn't want to be caught slipping.

We pulled up to a location that was just an empty lot, got out of the cars, and I looked around in anger.

"What the fuck am I looking at?" I got up in the dickless man's face. "Is this some type of trick?"

"I-I swear this was a huge house with multiple rooms for storage and processing of all types of drugs. I was just here a few days ago. It-it can't be gone."

I pulled out my gun and shot him in the head.

"Dispose of this dickless faggot."

I was more pissed off than before. I couldn't believe this shit. This ghost had a building demolished and removed in a matter of days. His flaunting of his ability to do what he wanted and not get caught only fueled my anger.

"This bitch must be stopped. I . . . want . . . what's . . . mine. This city belongs to *me!*" I raged as I drove away.

Chapter 13

Monica

Attention

Leroy came home mad last night—again. I was becoming tad bit less tolerable of his present behavior. He hadn't slept in our bed in over a week. It was either in the car, on the patio, or in his office. I didn't know how much more that I could take. I was a woman, and I had needs. I needed attention from my man, and plastic wasn't going to fulfill me at all. I wanted my flesh-and-blood husband to pleasure me like only he could.

I was soaking in a nice hot bath with body oils and bubbles surrounding me. I rubbed my legs together, and the silkiness of my own skin aroused me. I slipped my fingers in between my legs and fingered myself deeply and sensuously. My eyes were already closed, and I was ready to get myself where I longed to be: pleasured.

There was a knock on the door stopping me midstroke. Excitement immediately filled my mind and body.

"Who is it?" I asked, hoping it was my husband coming to the rescue. I think I purred down below as well.

"Ma, you still going with me to basketball practice today, right?" my son asked through the door. Immediately, disappointment dissolved all the excitement that I just had.

"Yeah, baby," I spoke as my body slid down in the tub a bit. I never thought I would be in this place. The needy-wife syndrome. I had it all, except my husband. "Give me a few minutes to get dressed, and we'll be out the door and on our way."

"Cool," was all he said, and then there was silence again. I was left alone with me and my thoughts. It's crazy how life can be picturesque one moment, and then the next, you're lost and don't know how you got there. I called my husband several times today, and all I got was "I'ma call you right back," "I'm handling some business," or the most hated . . . straight to voice mail. Like I said before, I never had to worry about my husband and another chick. He knew who he had at home. His mistress, the streets were never any competition . . . until now. He wanted it all, and I was already his, so I guess he wasn't worried about me leaving or venturing off. I felt the same way up until this moment. I needed attention. I craved it. I eased out of the tub, and then dried off. I prepped myself as I normally do with a little pizzazz added to my look this time. I wasn't going to cheat on my husband. A few glances and stares would give me the attention that I wanted right now.

Before I knew it, I was ready to go and enjoy the day. I walked down the steps and into the living room where my son was sitting with his back to me. He was texting as usual. That damn phone was a piece of his body. I swear I want to go back and look at his baby pictures and see if he had come out of the womb with it in his hand.

"I'm ready," I spoke, announcing my presence. Our house was almost completely carpeted so getting around in stealth mode was quite easy.

"Oh, hey, Ma." He looked startled, like I surprised him. He did a double take as he looked at me.

"Damn, Ma, where you going dressed like that?" His mouth hung open because he has never seen me dress in the manner that I was.

"*Excuse* me?" I looked at him with disapproval of his language and statement.

"I'm sorry, Ma, but you look like—" he quickly cut off himself from speaking any further.

"What do I look like?" I asked, curious for his response. I wanted attention from him as well.

"I was going to say you look different . . . yeah . . . different." He smiled.

"So is different bad or good?" I baited him.

"Ma, I'm not going there with you. That is a sucker move, for sure. I might as well tell you that you are fat or something. Not going to happen. So, you look different." He laughed.

"All right, I'll let you off the hook this time because I know that I am dressed, as you say, *different*. So, let's go so we won't be late. I don't want your coach hollering at me for showing up late like before," I laughed.

He got up; then we left. I can't help but say that I was excited to get out of the house even in the outfit that I had on. It was just a cute little sundress that highlighted my breasts and behind. I was normally a jeans-and-pants girl. I loved dresses, but I was a house mom, so running around in a dress was not my style. Today was a new day, I had some attention to get, and I was all for it.

I was so glad that after the first two practices my son's coach let the parents stay and watch them practice. I had very few girlfriends, and I lived a life catering to my family.

Anyway, there were some good-looking guys that brought their sons to practice as well. I didn't want them, but I wanted them to want me. I was going to be an attention whore today.

We walked into the gymnasium where the boys practice, and I walked with purpose. I had my pocketbook on my arm, and I sashayed as all the eyes, ladies included, followed me to my seat. Only about ten parents were in attendance, with me included, but they were mostly men.

"Ma, what was that walk for?" My son leaned over and whispered in my ear as I sat down.

"What walk?" I played dumb. "I was walking like a normal person, one foot in front of the other." I smiled as I looked over and saw a few eyes peering in my direction. I was elated at the attention that I was getting.

"Ma, that was *not* a normal walk. Ma, you walked like you, excuse my language, but like you shit yourself." He continued to whisper in my direction. I laughed on the inside but chastised him outwardly.

"Corey, mind your business and do what we came here to do." I looked at him, he shook his head and then moved down to the court to do his laps like before.

Practice flew by, and it was time to go. I was all filled up on attention by this time. Two men couldn't keep their eyes off me. One was bold enough to bring me a bottle of water even though he was the one that needed it. He damn near had his tongue hanging out of his mouth panting like a dog. It was about two hours' worth of practice, and I "went to the bathroom" several times. The women were jealous, and the men were drooling. I couldn't ask for more attention. I still wanted my husband's attention, though.

All the parents and boys were packing up and leaving. My son was the last one to leave. He was talking to the coach. I waited by the car for them to make their exit. He came out with the coach in tow.

I had to say that the coach was all about his business. His work ethic and attitude reminded me of my husband. But I could tell he wasn't on my husband's level. He was out here teaching boys to play ball. He was a blue-collar worker, for sure.

"Ma, Coach wants to take us out for dinner," Corey said with a smile. I personally didn't want to go, but he was getting some good lessons from this guy, and I didn't want to stifle the bond that I could see growing between the two.

"Sure, that would be nice," I spoke, and then smiled. I hope he had class and takes us somewhere without a drive-thru.

"We'll follow your lead," I politely spoke to Corey's coach. I felt bad because I didn't even know his name. I would make it a point to get to know his name. That would be the respectable thing to do.

When we pulled up to Panera, I was mildly excited. I liked the place, but it was just a bump up from McDonald's in my opinion. I would make it work, nonetheless.

Chapter 14

Corey

Inclinations

This guy kind of reminded me of my dad. You know, his aggressiveness for what he wants and not-taking-any-excuses attitude was my father's same style of living. In the few short practices that we have had, I was already thinking more like a leader and not a follower. My father had already been a great example. Now, my coach was filling in the gap with my father's consistent focus on building his empire. I wasn't mad at my father, just wish he would focus on his family more. I loved him nonetheless, though.

"So, Coach, what do people call you on a normal basis? You know, in a normal setting?" my mother asked. She had a look of curiosity. For some reason, my mother was on kick today. I wasn't sure what to expect next. I mean, my mother was a tough chick, but most of all, she was a laid-back chick. She stayed in the pocket and observed. I have never seen her this outgoing before. She was a drug dealer's wife for sure; unpredictable.

"People call me Mr. Clarence," he said with what looked like a glimmer of a smile in the corners of his mouth. That surprised me as well. This dude spewed hate and obscenities at us like we were common street trash just a few minutes ago. Now he was close to Mr. Rogers in this bitch.

"Well, Mr. Clarence, why in the hell are you treating my son and the other boys like shit most of the time?" she asked.

I looked at him and waited for the answer. I was curious as well. I mean, I could handle it, because my dad was hard core most of the time, with the language anyway. He was a "G," as they call it.

"Mrs. . . .?" He paused and waited for my mother to answer.

"Monica, Monica is my name."

"Well, Monica, I have to get to them before the world does. I know it's a little late in the game to try to mold some hard-headed boys, but I get in where I fit in. These boys need a strong hand to reinforce what their fathers and mothers may, or may not, have instilled in them. This world is a cold one, and no one cares for you once you get out there. Only the strong survive. The rest become victims of the strong or work for them. Your son won't have a problem. He is a king in the making. You and your husband have done a very good job with him. He has a good head on his shoulders, and he never backs down from a challenge. He's going to go far in his life. I guarantee it."

I was smiling inwardly and outwardly as he finished. My mother was as well. He was right. My parents did do a great job with me. I was destined for greatness. I just didn't know what for.

"If Corey stays humble and true to himself, then he will be just fine," he said as he looked in my direction. The smile disappeared from my face.

"I will," I spoke seriously.

"He is his father's son," my mother added. "I hope the apple didn't fall too far from the tree." She laughed a tad.

"Well, there is something different about Corey, and I just don't know what it is. He has a rough and tough temperament, but he can be compassionate at the same time. He is quite different from the other boys on the team. He doesn't have a point to prove. That's what I like about him. I think more will be revealed about him soon. I just can't wait to see it."

He had me nervous, now. So, nervous that I didn't and couldn't look at my mother in the face. Did this guy know my secret? He couldn't have. I had to change the subject and quickly.

"So, Coach, when do you think our first game will be?"

"With the way you guys are going, we'll be tournament ready in about two weeks. Just in time for the first game. I'm going to be stepping up the pace the next two weeks so we can be solid and a force to be reckoned with. With you on lead, we got this championship on lock. I love to win, and I hope that you do as well."

"I sure do," I said with enthusiasm. I have played soccer, hockey, football, and lacrosse, and dominated them all. Basketball will be added to my list of accomplishments.

We talked some more and ate some food. After about an hour, we left the restaurant, and then parted ways. On the way home, my mother decided that she wanted to grill me on Coach's curiosity.

"Is there something that you need to tell me?"

"What are you talking about, Ma? You know everything about me." I tried to sound reassuring. I was texting and on Facebook, not wanting to give her my full attention. It wasn't that serious to me now. I wished Coach would have kept his inclinations to himself. Now she was going to be all up in my business. I liked it when she was just an overprotective mother not a nosy one.

"Corey, I'm not a surprise type of a person. I will bust you in the ass if you bring some bullshit late in the game. I mean it."

"Ma, I'm cool. There's nothing you need to worry about. I'm good. I got this."

Suddenly, we were parked on the side of the road, and she was looking me in the side of my face. I could feel her eyes engrossed in me, like she wanted to strangle me. I didn't want to face her because she had a way of manipulating me with her eyes. I wasn't falling for it.

"Don't fucking play with me. What the hell is going on?" She got even closer to me and slapped my phone out of my hand. I truly almost lost it and fucked my mother up for that one, but I kept it cool. It was just a phone, and she did no harm to it anyway. I didn't want to heighten a situation that was already tense.

"You want to know the truth?" I looked her in the eyes as she did the same. We were in close proximity. Too close for my comfort, I might add.

"Everything," she said, her teeth clinched together.

"I got this chick pregnant and you about to be a grandma. You got two weeks," I spoke, and then turned and reached for my phone.

She was silent for a few moments. I was nervous because she didn't say anything. I looked back at her, and she just sat back in the driver's seat.

"Ma, I'm joking. There is no pregnant girl. I was just trying to get you off my back. You know everything you need to know about me. You're my mother. You know me already."

"Okay," was the only thing she said as she pulled off and back on to the road again. I was relieved and cognizant that this wasn't over. That wasn't a normal "okay." That was a "I will be on your ass every chance I get" okay. It was also an "I am a private detective/your momma" okay. This wasn't the first time with this. Now I had to be on my best behavior for a few days. That means no more gay porn or dirty sex talk on my phone. I didn't know what type of capabilities she had or the people she knew with those capabilities. I immediately started to delete shit from my phone. Most of the time my parents trusted me and left me to live my life. Now, suddenly, I would be on 24/7 surveillance.

Chapter 15

Clayton

Work of Art

I was cold and in awe. I was standing in the morgue for the state of Maryland. I was called down to look at a body that was found a few days ago in the back of an abandoned car.

In my line of work, I was never happy to be in the presence of the dead or decomposing bodies. We all had to die, I just didn't want to see it face-to-face all the time. I avoided it at almost every turn. But today was one of those times that I would have to bite the bullet and do what needed to be done.

I was outside of the room where the body I was about to see was staged. I was a man in all rights, but this just wasn't something I loved. But, again, it was necessary. I grabbed the jar of Vicks VapoRub to put a dab under my noise. It was to hinder me from smelling the decay in the room. My smell wasn't the only thing that I was worried about. It would be that the sight that I saw that would be forever etched into my memory. I didn't want to close my eyes and see a dead body for the next few nights.

I stood at the door, closed my eyes momentarily, and breathed in and out for a few seconds; then I put my hand on the swinging doors that looked like they could fit right into an animal slaughterhouse.

"Good day, Detective." I was greeted by a pasty-white female with a smile as bright as a sunny day. I wasn't the least bit jovial. "So glad you could come down today."

"No problem," I lied. I tried to put on a smile that matched hers, but it felt, and was, fake. It didn't last long either.

"Well, let's get right to work. I have something fascinating that I want to show you." I could feel the excitement oozing from her pores. You didn't have to be a rocket scientist to see that she loved her job. I almost rolled my eyes.

"Sure." I followed behind her as she walked over to a table with a body that was covered with a white sheet.

"Get ready to say bravo to this work of art."

This bitch was way too excited.

She removed the sheet as if she were Houdini himself, and this was her magic act.

The body on the table was decomposing, but it was still in very good shape, if you can say that about a dead body.

"This just . . ." I said and then paused. I was in awe and speechless.

"I know. I said the same thing when he first came in. I heard that this was one of the victims that you were looking for. That mysterious drug dealer guy did this to him, right?" She looked very curious to get an answer.

"I-I don't . . . I think so." I looked on in disbelief. I knew that this was one of the victims of the Ghost, but I didn't and couldn't give out that type of information to her. I didn't know if she could be trusted, and some information just wasn't available to the public, and she was, technically, the public.

"It is. I know it is. I've been following these cases and things related to it. I know some people and—"

"This stays in this room," I spoke, cutting her off. "You will be brought up on charges if this gets out. I promise."

She looked at me like she was a scolded child, but I didn't care. She wasn't about to fuck up my work and possible increase in the ranks.

I walked around the table a few times taking in as much as I could. I took out my phone and took a few pictures of the body. The plastic surgery work on the body was exquisite. It *was* a work of art. You would have thought that this body had come out of the womb this way. Everything was just so seamless and perfect. The scarring was almost unnoticeable. You had to be close to this body to even tell. Whoever did this to this person was a master. This ghost guy was on point in every aspect.

I left after I was done with my evidence. All I could think about on the drive home was the fact that this guy had the best of the best in the streets and doing his dirty work. How was I going to catch him?

Chapter 16

Avery

Human

I am not invincible or untouchable. I just go unnoticed. It's the way that I like it. I'm the average person with some heightened senses. On average, a person does not pay attention to their surroundings. We watch things, but we don't pay attention. I take notes about other people and their actions and compare them to my own. I have been that way ever since I can remember. I'm human in every way, shape, and form. I just conform to the people's perceptions around me at any given time. I am who you think I am at that given time. Right at this moment, these boys see me as their coach. Later, I will be a kingpin running an empire that practically runs itself. Like most businesses, chain stores especially, you need workers that need money. You place someone in charge that is more in need of money and things; then you supply them with instructions and goals.

Everyone loves a challenge. We lie and say we want things to be easy, but no one does. We want to prove that we have earned our keep. And then there is fear and expectation. Those two will keep most, not all, loyal. Then you have examples of disciplinary actions toward the ones without loyalty. Because, again, there will always be one or two that will try your hand. Throw in some incentives and advancements and you have yourself a well-oiled machine that only needs to be tended and given maintenance when needed. Sure, they have some challenges, but it comes with the territory.

The truth is, I'm lonely. As the saying goes, it gets lonely at the top. I hadn't had companionship in a long time. And in this game, you can't trust anyone, even the ones you trust, if that makes sense. I make tons of money, but I only spend it on myself and a few charities, anonymously. I couldn't showboat because money brings attention, and the attention is followed by leeches and parasites called friends and family.

I was in my car driving around thinking about Corey and his mom. They seemed like a good family from the looks of things and the way they carried themselves. It made me a little envious.

I decided to take a drive around my old neighborhood. My family still lives in the same house that I grew up in. I wasn't an only child, but it felt like it most of my life. I was the one that strayed away and isolated myself. The world made me do it. The projection and rejection of the gay black male in society had me doomed from the start. Once I realized what I was, in their eyes, I withdrew myself and closed myself off from my family. I wasn't abused, molested, or talked down to by my family. It was television and the neighborhood that pushed me away with its idea of what gay life was. It was like I didn't have a chance from the beginning. Don't feel sorry for me because I'm cool with me now. I know that I'm not a germ. I'm a gem. Sometimes I just wish that I could go back and spare my parents the heartache of me running away and disappearing in the shadows. It's easy to get lost in this city and still be in plain sight. I've been playing invisible most of my life. Hide-and-seek was my life.

I drove down the block I lived and played on for a short time, and all the pain and memories flooded back into my mind. I wanted a do over. I wanted to go back and scream out to the world that I wasn't a germ, and then live the life that most other people lived. But that wasn't going to happen. I was fully immersed in the life I lived now. I was happy by most standards, but it didn't hurt to have regrets.

I slowed down a little to see some people sitting on the porch of the row house I once lived in. I watched the world destroy me before I had a chance . . . right from that porch. There was a gay boy that lived on the block as well. He knew who I was, and I him, but neither of us said a word. The other boys and girls in the neighborhood that we played with on a regular basis made his life a living hell daily. I vowed that it would never be me every time I witnessed something done to him. The boy would take anything to keep them as friends. The girls would make him wear dresses and makeup, and the boys would taunt him relentlessly afterward. The abuse was acceptable just as long as they were his friends. If friendship was like that, then I didn't want it. That was my vow. To never want to experience that type of abuse on any level.

On the steps was an older man and woman. I knew who they were. They were my parents. They looked older but just like I remember them. One day I just may go up and hug them, but the pain was too hard for me to bear. This would be enough for me. I take this stroll every so often to check up on them. My windows were tinted, so my identity was protected. I also had some plastic surgery done, so even if they saw me, they would never recognize me. I went to great lengths to maintain my life and secrecy.

I moved on down the block to see business going on that made me richer by the day. I continued on my way. I grabbed myself a bite to eat, and then returned to the shadows of my life.

Chapter 17

Leroy

Father's Day

I sat down at the strip club with my boy, my seed. I was a proud guy. To find out that your son was banging broads' backs out was a thing a father loved to here. Fuck what you heard, every man wanted to hear that their son is a ladies' man. I got a chance to sit down and talk to my wife, something I haven't done in a minute because of my preoccupation with my empire. She said she had some suspicions about Corey's sexual habits and that as his father, I needed to investigate. She didn't want to be a grandmother this early in her life, and I need to check him before she gives him a homemade vasectomy. My wife was my twin when it came to the tongue and mindset. It was one of the many things that attracted me to her, along with that fat ass of hers.

"Corey, you out here spreading them wild oats like it's no problem?"

"What?" He looked at me like I shouldn't have asked that question. "Nah, it ain't that type of party."

"Come on, dude, the wife said that you were hiding some shit and it was about a girl being pregnant and shit. Give me the business on that." I looked at him with pride and curiosity. I didn't want him to be a father this early either, but I wasn't going to browbeat him for doing something natural. A man had to be a man. Fucking broads was protocol . . . a man's world.

"Pop, Moms bugging and shit. I was just joking around with her, and she took things to the left on me. I told her it was a joke, and she didn't believe me. I straps up anyway when I getting that ass. I'm team 'no-kids' right now."

I couldn't help but laugh. The language that the young boys use nowadays was wild and unpredictable, but I could relate. I didn't strap up when I was having sex with his mom, and that's why we're sitting at this table together now.

"Corey, that's all I needed to hear. I'll reassure your moms when we get home. Now, let's get rid of some of this money. These hoes in here looking like they're thirsty, and I got the cure for that thirst." He laughed, and so did I. I didn't cheat on my wife and had no need to either. She had this dick on lock. It didn't mean I couldn't admire what God created every so often, though. It was something that I did when I wanted to clear my mind, and now being that my son was with me, I could have fun.

Chapter 18

Monica

Monica 101

"I am not going to take this shit much longer." I was in my garden trying to get some peace of mind. My garden was one of my hiding places out in the open. It was in our close-to-a-quarter-acre backyard. I had a wooden gazebo made with a swing that sat in the middle of the garden. The garden was filled with my perennials and annuals. I had two small cement benches on both sides of the gazebo for resting in between clipping and pruning my precious flowers. I had a bottle of wine with me to help me pass the time, as well. This was my other pastime when I didn't go shopping. This was another way to save money too. I tended to shop heavy and ended up buying clothing that I probably will never wear. I took a few more sips from my glass and then filled it back up again. I planned on getting drunk before the day was over.

My husband and my son were about to drive me crazy with all their craziness. Late nights out, and then attitude when questioned was not a good look for me. I was trying to hold this family together, and no one was the slightest bit concerned about me. There was only so much a down chick could take. I was at my wit's end with Corey and Leroy. I needed and wanted to get out of the house. But I didn't have any friends to call on, and I was an only girl, so calling my brothers was like talking to brick walls. They were somewhat insensitive at times. They weren't totally coldhearted, but they were street-bred guys. They left their feelings on the dresser in their homes. I didn't want to get them involved anyway. Both of my parents were dead, so that left me basically alone.

I stayed in the garden for close to two hours sipping and clipping, and I was tired of clipping, so I came in the house. I flopped down on my living-room sofa. I was more tired from stressing than I was of clipping and pruning flowers. I picked up my phone off the coffee table that was in front of the sofa that I was resting on and began to scroll through the contacts hoping that I could find someone to talk to about anything. Let's just say there was slim pickings. Everybody was in the life. Except one person. Corey's coach. I knew that it was a long shot, but I was desperate for attention right now. He seemed like an interesting guy at the restaurant the other day, so why not get to know the person that had potential to shape parts of Corey's mind differently than his father and I? At least, that's what half of the bottle of wine I just drank in the garden told me. They say that alcohol was liquid courage. With it, you could do and say anything that you normally would not do or say. This was one of those moments.

I pushed the call button next to his name and waited for him to pick up on the other side of the phone. I was tempted to hang up after a few rings, but he picked up before I could do so.

"Hello."

His deep voice made me a little nervous. I didn't know why because I was used to guys with deep voices. I think it was the desperation that made me nervous.

"I'm sorry for calling you . . . I mean, this is something I never do," I stammered.

"If you do it once, including now, that takes the word 'never' out of the picture." He spoke in an even and self-assured voice.

"Well . . . uh . . ." I paused, at a loss for words.

"Monica, is everything okay with Corey?"

"Who?" I sounded so absentminded.

"Corey, your *son*," he reminded me. There was a small laugh that followed his statement.

"Oh, Lord. Yes, he's fine. I think. I hope." I blew out a frustrated breath.

"I take it you are not sure of his whereabouts and you were wondering if I knew anything?" he estimated.

"No, that's not the reason why I'm calling you. I wasn't concerned about his whereabouts now. I know that he is capable of handling himself. He's his father's son, for sure."

"Oh, okay. What can I do for *you*, then?" he asked. The silence on the other end was scary. He was waiting for an answer that I wasn't sure of right now. What *could* he do for me?

"To be honest, Coach, I'm not really sure of why I called."

"I see."

"I'm bored at home, and there was nobody that I could really talk to that would be unbiased if I needed to talk."

"Well, that's great. I'm glad that you trusted me enough to consider calling me. It's an honor."

"I hope that you aren't busy." We had already been on the phone for a minute or so now. I guess it was crazy to ask if he was busy or not.

"Monica, I was not doing a thing. Mainly thinking and planning in my head. You know, world domination." He laughed, and I followed in the same manner. If this was his way of lightening up the mood on my end, it had worked.

"Boy, do I know about that." I went back into my thoughts about my crazy and dedicated husband and all his plans for the takeover of Baltimore City.

"Anything you say to me is between us. I'm a very private person myself. You can trust me."

"I don't know why, but I believe you." I paused, and then went right into my thoughts. "Well, Coach, my husband is a very busy man, and he is almost always busy at work for these last few weeks. I mean, I'm used to him being busy, but usually there was time for us to get together and do husband-and-wife things. Now, I'm lucky if I get a kiss on the forehead. A woman has needs, you know. I'm just feeling rejected right now and lonely. How do you think I can get my husband's attention?"

"Well, Monica, that's a hard question to answer. I'll ask you this, though. Have you spoken to your husband about this issue?"

"Yes. He's not totally neglecting me. It's just not what it used to be. His passion for success has surpassed his passion for me. I used to be his number one priority. Now, I feel like one of the boys in a dress."

"Well, Monica, I say you force him to sit down and have a talk. Make it plain that this is not good for your relationship and put your needs on the table. You may have to give him an ultimatum."

"Oh, hell no," I belted out, and then laughed at the thought. "My husband is *not* that kind of man. That wouldn't work in my favor at all. I don't know what to do."

"Monica, the only thing I can think of is if you show him what he's missing. A man loves a hands-on lesson. Take him back to school with Monica 101. He needs to be reeducated on the needs of a lady, especially *his* lady. I have to go now. I need to handle some business, but let me know what happens. Talk to you later."

He hung up the phone without even letting me say good-bye. It wasn't necessary, though. I had got what I needed, and I hoped that it would work.

Chapter 19

Corey

A Tight Situation

My mother let me have the car so that I could take care of some business like I said that I wanted to, but the whole time driving, it felt like I was being followed. I knew that my mother had talked to my father about the "pregnancy situation," and he interrogated me as well. Then he put one of his boys on my trail. I was pissed because I wanted to go get me a piece of ass, and this was blowing me. I hated being a part of a drug family at times like these. My father was on his hyperprotective bullshit, and now I was being trailed. It was so-called protection, but the only protection that I needed right now was the Trojan condom I was about to use to go up into some fresh ass.

I was becoming more and more pissed as I drove closer and closer to my destination. I had to do some ditching to get this fucker off my tail. It wouldn't be easy because my father had some loyal guys, and they did what he said . . . or they didn't come back.

It was later at night, and the streets that I was taking were busy. I began weaving in and out of traffic, and then speeding up, and this dude was still on me. He knew that I knew he was following me. He made it a point to show me. I hated that shit. I even ran a few lights to see if he would follow, and sure enough, he was right on me. He was intentionally trying to fuck up my night. That shit worked.

I finally pulled over in a quiet neighborhood, and this dude had the nerve to park a few cars up like he wasn't following me. I quickly hopped out of my car and sprinted to his car.

"Stop following me, yo." I mean mugged him. I was still my father's son and heir to his throne. I had some pull.

"Little dude, I'm on assignment. There is nothing you can do or say to get me off your tail."

"Dude, I'm on some private shit, and I need you to get lost for a few. How much you want to get missing for a few?"

"Dude, you ain't got what I want. I'm good." He looked serious.

"Dude, you mean to tell me that if I got a chick to fuck your brains out for free, you wouldn't take a break on trailing me?"

"Dude, pussy's overrated. Your pops serious about his seed. I'm on you till you make it home."

"Damn, I can't believe you turning down some pussy for my pops. He can't be paying you that much."

"It's about loyalty. Not money." He looked at me expressionless. He was a regular guy's height with some muscle. Damn, dude was good looking too.

His phone rang, and he answered it. He had a few words with whoever was on the phone; then he hung up and set it on one of his legs. He had one of those huge phones that could be a phone and a tablet.

My eyes caught hold of a very familiar app that was very risqué to have in my father's clique. This was an app that I had on my phone, but it was hidden. This dude must have two phones, and that phone probably was his personal one. He was slipping because he was driving all alone. I guess my father had some of his other men on other assignments.

"Dude, I guess you're right. Pussy is overrated, but dick must be right up your alley."

"Li'l bro, saying that could get you killed." He looked at me like it was a threat on my life.

"Especially if my father found out that one of his boys liked boys. Kind of crazy to hear him talk about you in that manner and keep your composure."

"Dude, you got the wrong one." He was sticking to his story firmly.

"That app on your phone says something else. I know what it's all about. All I need to do is make a call to my dad and your life is over. I don't think you want that."

"What you want from me?" he asked, finally giving in.

"I want some of your ass." I smiled at the irony of the situation. I was going to get some ass when, all along, some ass was following me. I know what you're thinking. I'm taking a chance at this dude spilling the beans on me about my sexuality too. But I figured my father would kill him first. Worst-case scenario for me is my father disowning me. But I doubt if it would ever get that far. I would kill dude before it ever moved past his lips.

He looked at me like he was confused.

"Yeah, man, I'm gay, and you will be able experience some of this good ole dick. Keep this between us and I won't have to spill the beans."

"Cool," was all he said as he nodded. I had to admit, he was easy to persuade. I guess dick and pussy reigned. It just depends on who you talking to.

"Follow me," I said, and then walked back to my car.

It didn't take long before we were at secluded motel. My anticipation was off the charts. I had him book the room; then we made our way in.

He was a little hesitant as he walked in front of me. This may have been his first time.

"This your first time?" I asked as we stood in the middle of the small room.

"With someone your age, yes." He looked like he was ashamed. He had to be in his late thirties, and I was still in high school.

"Dude, age ain't nothing but a number. You going to enjoy this dick." I grabbed my already pulsating dick through my sweatpants. "Get on them knees and get that throat ready to be stretched."

He did as he was told, and I pulled my dick out and let it hang out over the waistband of my pants. His eyes got big with excitement. He moved in for the kill. The warmth of his mouth was out of this world. I had a blow job before, but dude was going to town. He was sucking so hard on my dick that I lost my footing a few times.

"Let's get these off. Take your shit off too." I removed my pants, and he did the same. He had a big dick as well and a nice fat ass that was hidden in the loose-fitting jeans he had on.

I sat down on the bed, and he got back on his knees and began to deep throat me like he was an Olympic dick sucker going for the gold medal.

His phone rang, and he immediately stopped what he was doing. He put his hand up to silence me. I wasn't a moaner, so that wasn't a problem anyway.

He answered the phone. "Hey, sir. Yes, I'm still on him. He stopped at this offbeat motel with some girl in the car. It looks like they are going to be in there for a while. No, sir, I will not leave for anything. Yes, I will let you know when they are finished and when he is home safe . . . later."

He hung up the phone; then he got back to giving me some throat sex.

"Damn, dude, you good at this shit. I just might make you my bitch. Now get up on that bed on all fours I want to feel them walls around my dick."

I grabbed my pants and took a condom out of the back pocket. I strapped it on my dick and primed his ass for my girth. I lubed up my finger and his ass with my saliva and eased in a finger at a time until he was riding three of my fingers with ease. He let out a few whimpers that made me rock hard. I loved a guy who made some noise to let me know they were enjoying the sex.

I eased up behind him, and then slowly eased myself into him. He wiggled and thrust himself toward my lap like an experienced dick rider. I was loving it. It didn't take long before the slapping of skin could be heard. I fucked hard, and then slow. I didn't want to come too soon. I wanted to enjoy it, and I wanted him to enjoy it to. Fucking him doggie style was cool, but I loved to fuck on my side.

He was throwing himself back giving me the fucking of my life. He had experience. This wasn't my first time, but most of the guys I have fucked were a little timid and scared. He wasn't at all.

Dre and I fucked for over an hour; then he followed me back home like he promised my father. He gave me his private number so that we could get together again. I was looking forward to it too. When I fell asleep, I slept like a contented baby.

Chapter 20

Avery

Playing Games

It's amazing the influence that you can have on people if you got what they needed. All you need to have is an answer to one of their problems; then you have them in the palm of your hands.

Monica was a beautiful woman, and her husband was too busy chasing a ghost to realize it. Yes, I knew who these people are. Her husband was the main man trying to find me to take me down. What were the odds that this situation would fall into my lap? Well, the odds were good, because I sent the invitation to their house inviting their son to play basketball on my team. I knew my enemy well, yet he knew little about me. I wanted to play the cat-and-mouse game for a little bit before I destroyed him and his family. I had his son and now his wife. I wanted to see if she was a strong advocate for her husband as she says and acts as if she is. I was getting bored because running a drug and crime business was boring after a while. To me, that is. Once again, it gets lonely at the top. So, I had to invent some games along the way to amuse myself. Yes, these were lives of people that I was playing with, but I didn't care. They knew the consequences of getting into the game. Besides, who needs family anyway? I didn't have my own, and I was thriving in life. Sure, I get lonely from time to time, but it passes, and so will it when I break this family apart.

"So, what's your home life like, Corey?" I asked. He was in my office, and it was right after we had practiced hard for our first game in a few days. I had certificates and trophies that were in a lighted case on the wall opposite of me and pictures of past teams posted on the walls to my left and right. My dark cherry wood desk was in pristine order and shining as if it was brand new. The sunlight from the window behind hit it and added to the quality of the desk.

Corey was still sweaty and glistening on his shoulders and chest. He was a fine specimen, and I'm sure the ladies and boys were all over him. I'm sure he would only confess to the ladies, though. He didn't know that I knew about his sexuality. He was too much like me at his age. He hid it well. I knew all the signs because I was once where he is right now. I can imagine the turmoil going on in his life right at this time. His mother may have an inkling, but his father is totally clueless that he had the enemy right behind the closed doors where he sleeps. It was quite humorous to witness.

"It's pretty normal," he answered. He looked at me straight in the eyes. He was an honest liar, for sure. I loved it.

"You're an only child?" I asked. I knew the answer. I just wanted to bond with him so I could use him later.

"Yep, it's just me," he spoke nonchalantly.

"So you don't want any other brothers or sisters?" I inquired.

"My parents knew that I was the best and that there was no need to have any more children. I'm all they need." He spoke with confidence. I feel some arrogance mixed in with it. He was sure of himself. I liked it. It slightly reminded me of myself. I could control mine, though. I'll be teaching him how to very soon. I think that I'm going to make him my son. His father didn't appreciate him anyway. He probably tried to force his masculine ways down his throat just like most men in society. That's why they can't catch me. They feed me the bullshit through the media, and I used it to take down the city. They were at my mercy.

"So, if your mother told you that she was pregnant, what would you say?"

"They not getting it in like they used to, so that's not going to happen." Corey's confidence was on blast. He had some information too.

"Oh, but I bet that you are. You have a girlfriend?"

"Nope, but I have options," he answered, and then laughed lightly.

"What do you mean by 'options'?" I asked. I already knew that he was avoiding the question with the answer that he just gave. It was a good one too. An uninformed person would have taken it as he was a player and had many women, but I knew that it meant 'mind your own fucking business.'

"I meant it like I said it. Options. I get to choose. You know . . . options." He was sticking with that answer, and I knew that I would be testing him on these 'options' soon enough.

"So I take it your hand gets in a lot of work."

"My hand?" he looked confused for a second. Then it must have hit him. "Ohhhh shit. Dude, you are fucking crazy. You on some wild shit." He laughed and hit his hand on his leg as if I told a funny joke. He was getting comfortable with me. It was like a potter molding some clay. First, you had to massage it and get it in a place where you can mold it.

"Well, you did say options. So, I figured that was one of your 'options,'" I spoke, and then smiled.

"Well, I don't have to use that option that often . . . If you get my drift."

"Oh, I get your drift. But I would caution you to take your time with your options. Be careful and be you. Don't let anyone take that away from you. You have the freedom to be you. Fuck anybody that gets in your way. Got it?"

"Yes, I got it, Coach." He looked me in the eyes, and I did the same. Then he pulled his phone out and looked at it.

"I got to be going, Coach. My mom is outside waiting for me. It's been real," he said as he reached over to shake my hand. I wanted to pull him into an embrace and hug him like he was my son already, but that would soon become a reality in time.

Chapter 21

Leroy

Turned Off

It was about a quarter of eleven when I pulled up to my house. I was exhausted. Mostly mentally, though. Staying in the game and climbing to the top was exhausting. There was always money to be made and enemies to be stamped out. I hadn't been in the house this early in a long time. All I wanted to do is get in the shower and then get into bed. I prayed and hoped that I got a rest-filled sleep. I stepped out of the car and then walked up the stone path that led to the front door. I stopped and looked up at the house that the money I had made afforded me, and then looked around at the cars that I had and admired it all. I had it built on close to half an acre of land, unlike what I had as a child. I wanted my family to have this. It was two stories of hard work and tears. Three bedrooms, because we were planning on expanding the family, two-and-a-half baths, a two-car garage, and a fenced-in quarter-acre backyard. I didn't want to lose it to this ghost freak. I worked fucking hard to get it, and I had to work harder to keep it. I left the hood and promised my wife that we would never go back. I would die before I went back, and that was a promise I made to myself. Fear and rage filled up in me, and I didn't like it. I shook my head, trying to shake the thoughts of losing all of this and the respect of my family all to one man.

I finally opened the door to my home and breathed a sigh of relief. I felt safe in the confines of my home. They say a man's home is his castle, and I agreed 100 percent.

It was dark in the house when I entered it. I could hear the television on upstairs. Monica needed some sounds from the television to help her sleep. I didn't need it and preferred not to have anything on because I needed to be aware of my surroundings and odd sounds. I was hoping Monica was asleep so that I could move about without her questioning me. She may have questions that I didn't have answers to, and I didn't want to be put in that position with my wife, along with ones I had myself about my current situation. She texted me earlier that day asking me about my expected arrival time home. I was glad that I didn't have to overanalyze anything my wife does because that could have been her keeping tabs on me if she was creeping out on me, but I had a loyal wife, and I didn't lose any sleep in that area. She knew who her king was. And my queen knew her place in my life. We had a bond that no one could break, and I didn't ever have to worry about it.

I walked up the steps to the second floor of our home, down the hallway, and headed straight to the bathroom that was on the outside of our bedroom. This is the one that Corey uses because we have one that is attached to our bedroom. I admired the decorations that lined the walls as I made my way down the hallway. My wife had good taste with African figurines and pictures hanging from the walls. It's amazing how much you pay attention when your way of living is threatened. With every step, I made sure that I didn't wake my wife. We didn't have squeaking floors, but I was just being extracautious. I needed to take a quick shower and then hop into bed. I had more meetings in the morning. My life was just one big meeting. The streets were watching, and they were waiting for the rightful king of the streets to take his place at the top.

I stripped down out of my clothes and turned the shower on. I let it run for a few seconds before I stepped in. I closed my eyes as I let the showerhead rinse the stress of the day away. I felt a presence behind me causing me to become defensive very fast. I turned around quickly, and before I knew it, I had my wife's body pinned to the back of the shower wall with my hand around her neck. The look on her face was of pure shock. I instantly released her and then apologized. "Damn, baby, I am so sorry. You scared the shit out of me. You were quiet as shit."

"I . . . I was just . . . just trying to take a shower with you. I wasn't trying to scare you." She looked at me in surprise as her chest heaved up and down.

"You know I would never hurt you, right?" I smoothed my hand on the side of her cheek with gentleness. I had to recover this situation. I hated being this aggressive and defensive, especially toward my wife. She was the last person I wanted to hurt.

"Yeah, Leroy. I know." She smiled, but I could tell that she was hurt by what just happened. Anyone would be hurt, especially if this was the *second* time that it happened. I kicked myself mentally.

"Good," I spoke, and then asked, "Monica, could you wash my back for me? A brother is tired."

"Sure, baby, I always have your back."

It stung a bit to hear her say that, but I ignored it. I knew that I needed to pay more attention to her. She was one of the main ones that I pushed on the back burner when I decided to take this guy's hold he had on the city. I would make it up to her when it was over.

We were out of the shower and in the bed within twenty minutes. I apologized to her several more times, hoping that she knew that I was sorry. I truly was sorry.

I was turned on my side trying to doze off, and the things of the day were running a race through my mind. I just wanted to rest. Monica didn't have those plans now. She eased up toward me and reached around me and eased her hands down my boxers and began to massage my manhood. It was feeling good, but I just didn't have the energy or the willingness to participate in any sexual activities. Sex took work, and even if she rode me like a cowgirl, I still would have to act like I was into it. My libido was gone now. I carefully moved her hand off my dick and over back toward her. I felt bad, but I would feel even worse if I participated halfheartedly.

"Not tonight, Monica. I just want to get some sleep."

There was silence on her end, but I did feel her turn over in the bed. I turned over too and moved up close to her and put my arms around her.

"Baby, you know I love you, right?" I whispered in her ear.

"Mm-hmm," she said as she nodded her head.

"I just need some time to get this business taken care of; then we'll go away. Just the two of us. I love you, Monica."

"I love you too, Leroy."

I turned back over and proceeded to get some rest.

Chapter 22

Monica

Unstable

As soon as I heard the light snores of my husband I sobbed quietly to myself. I had to admit that I was hurt. Deeply hurt. My husband wasn't the man I married right now. I don't know when exactly he changed, but I knew that I was not happy with it at all. He has never put his hands on me until now, even if he did say it was the pressure of the streets or the fact that I startled him. In my mind, he was unstable. And now, I felt like I was as well. My whole family felt unstable right now, as a matter of fact.

How can I fix this? Can we come back from this? Is this the way that it's supposed to be? I wrestled with these questions in my mind as I lay there beside a man I no longer knew now. Soon, I pulled the covers off myself and made my way out of the bedroom and down to the kitchen. I needed a snack or something to ease my mind.

As I made my way down the steps, Corey was coming in the house.

"Hey, baby." I gave him a faint smile as I walked up to him and gave him a tight hug. I pulled away, and then made my way toward the kitchen.

"Ma, what's wrong with you?" he asked as he trailed behind me toward the kitchen.

"Nothing, I'm good, baby," I spoke as I opened the refrigerator and peered inside to see what I could grab for a quick snack. I purposely didn't look at him when I answered him. I was wearing my anguish, and he would read it right away if he saw my face at this moment. My legs were threatening to give way to the floor at any moment now.

"Ma, that is some bull." He came over to me and aggressively turned me around. At that moment, I was too weak and vulnerable to chastise the way he talked to me and handled me. The tears that I was holding back instantly fell like a cascading waterfall when he lifted my head so that I was looking him in the face.

"What the fuck happened?" The anger in his voice was fairly evident. He shook me a little like I was a rag doll. I was shocked that he was handling me this way.

"Corey, let me go." I spoke aggressively but in a low tone. He did as I requested. I retreated to a chair at the table that was in the middle of the kitchen. I put my elbows on the table, and then put my face in my hands.

I rubbed my face feverishly trying to get myself together. I heard Corey pull out a chair that was close to me. He then put his hand on my shoulder. "Ma, what's going on?" He had a better tone than a minute ago. It was loving and caring this time.

"Your father . . ." I spoke with my forehead still in my hands.

"Something happen to Daddy?" he asked. There was a little uneasiness that could be heard in his voice. He loved his father very much.

"No, he's fine. I guess." I spoke, and then I finally lifted my head up.

"You guess?" he looked at me in bewilderment. "Ma, what's going on?"

"Your father is upstairs sleeping peacefully." There was a hint of scorn in my voice that he didn't get nor would he understand.

"So, what's the problem?" he asked as he sat back in the chair. He looked to be more at ease.

"Your father has changed. He's not the same."

"Ma, you're losing me. Where is all of this coming from?"

"Your father and I had an episode earlier. It's nothing." I tried to sound convincing and unscathed by the events that happened earlier.

"What type of episode?" he asked. Tension made its way back into his body as he asked the question. I always asked for him to be honest with me, so I knew that I had to do the same thing with him. At times, I hated the rules I set for him, knowing that I would have to be a partaker of the same rules. It was moments like this that I hated being an adult.

"Well, I snuck into the shower with your father in it. I caught him by surprise, and he slammed my body into the wall with his hand around my neck. It didn't last but a few seconds, Corey. He apologized profusely. I forgave him."

"You have *got* to be fucking kidding me. This is the *second* time he did this shit. This shit is going to stop today." He stood up and marched toward the steps. I sprinted behind him and grabbed him by the arm.

"Corey, don't do anything. I got this," I pleaded softly. I didn't want any shit to go down in my house that may involve the police. Even though our family drug business is not run out of the house, we didn't want to draw any attention toward us. My son was not a small guy, but I managed to hold him back for a minute. "Corey, *please.*"

"Ma, that's the second time he put his hands on you 'by accident.' That is a load of shit."

"I know what it looks like, Corey, but your father is really going through something right now. I need you to stand down and let me handle this. This is *my* husband."

"I don't care, Ma, you're a woman. A man is not supposed to be hitting on a woman for *any* reason." He fumed as he looked up the steps. I prayed that he would listen to my voice.

"Corey, you are absolutely right. There is no excuse, but please let me handle this. *Please.*"

"Ma, this is the last time that this happens. Next time, I'm laying him down. Father or not." I let his arm go and then proceeded to make my way back in the kitchen. He followed me like I prayed that he would. He pulled out a chair and sat at the table. He watched me as I fumbled around the kitchen trying to get us something to nibble on together. I had to admit that my mind was all over the place.

I fixed us a late-night snack of grilled cheese and french fries. We ate in silence. I feared for my son and my husband. I prayed to God that my husband doesn't have another one of his 'episodes,' and even more, I prayed that my son is nowhere around if it does happen again.

"Corey, in life, we all have challenges, and sometimes those challenges bring out other personalities that are less favorable. Just like those curse words that flew out of your mouth when you got angry." I eyed him as he bit into his sandwich.

"I'm sorry, Ma," he apologized after he swallowed that bite he just took of his food. "I was bugging, but that's no excuse. I was supposed to think before I responded."

"Son, you get a pass this time, but next time, I just might bust your behind." A smile followed the statement, but I was totally serious.

We sat and talked for close to an hour before we both retired to our beds for some much-needed rest.

Chapter 23

Corey

No Mercy

I woke up the next morning with my mother and father still on my brain. I was still pissed. I told my mother that I would let her handle it, but in the back of my mind, my father was the enemy until further notice. My mom was off-limits to any and every one when it came to anything negative. I got out of my bed after a few minutes of just lying there. I quickly showered and made my way down the steps. It was still early in the morning. I heard my parents talking as I made my way into the kitchen.

"Hey, Ma." I leaned over and gave her a kiss on the cheek. I then made my way over to the refrigerator to retrieve some milk for the cereal that I was about to eat.

"So your pops don't get a good morning?" he asked. I hadn't even looked his way or acknowledged him yet. Yep, I was still heated.

"Sorry, Pop, just got something on my mind. You know how it is," I said as I sat down at the table. We had breakfast like this most of the time, but today was different. I wanted to break this ceramic bowl into my father's face and watch the blood drizzle down his chin. But I kept it cool and cordial. He was still my father no matter how bad I felt about him at this moment.

"Son, I know all about it. So how is the basketball thing going?"

"It's cool," I said in between a spoonful of Cinnamon Toast Crunch. I didn't have many words for him now. And here he was pretending that he cared. His ass hasn't been to not one of my practices, and he used to be at all my games when I played other sports. It's amazing how things have changed. Now my mom was there, and he was handling his business. I wasn't knocking him for handling business for his family, but at least take some time to spend it with us. An hour or two wasn't going to derail your plans.

"Your mother said that the coach is a lot like me; persistent and unrelenting."

"Yeah, he all right." I just wanted to get up and get the hell out of here.

"That's good to hear. Give them other teams hell and don't ever back down. You got my blood running through you, so I know dominating and handling your business," he boasted proudly. I could care less about anything he said now.

"Ma, I'ma be out back practicing. Let me know when you're ready to go." I got up from the table, put away the milk, placed my dishes in the sink, and walked out of the room.

I didn't even say good-bye to my father as I left the room. How dare he act as if nothing was wrong! Man, he can kick rocks with no shoes on for all I care.

It didn't take long for him to leave and for us to do the same. Don't get it twisted. I still loved and honored my dad, I just didn't like how he did things sometimes. He was on some new shit, and this obsession has taken over his life.

I practiced extra hard, and it showed because my entire practice uniform was completely drenched when we finished up.

I found myself in the coach's office again as I waited for my mother to come and scoop me up. She usually waits around until I finished, but today, she said she wanted to go shopping and that she would meet me back here when it was time for me to leave.

"So what's going on with you today?" Coach asked as he came in and sat down at his desk.

"I don't understand." I looked at him in confusion.

"You played really sloppy today and too hard. You were making way too many mistakes. I don't like mistakes, especially sloppy ones. Did I make a mistake in making you a captain?"

"No, sir, I thought I was doing just fine."

"I wanted to fuck you up several times today for that foolishness. But I thought I would question you before I tore into your ass. I decided to give you a bit of mercy. It doesn't happen often."

I looked at him like he was crazy for a moment. This dude has no fucks to give at all. He is straight to the point—always. If this was mercy he was giving me, I felt sorry for his enemies.

"Coach, I have some things on my mind, that's all. I was just going through some things, but that's no excuse for my performance today."

"It's understandable but unacceptable. Leave all that shit you going through outside the door before you walk through those doors. I don't care about your problems and neither will your opponents in life. This world takes no prisoners, so don't give it a chance to make you one."

I soaked up all that he was saying. He had a point, and he sounded a lot like my father.

"Coach, you have any children?"

He looked at me for a few seconds and then spoke. "Why?"

"I was just curious."

"Is that information going to advance you in any way?" he asked.

"Well . . . I—"

"No, the hell it won't," he cut me off. "That information is not going to advance you in *any* way. You don't need to know any fucking thing about me but the fact that I own your ass on this court and this team. Any more questions?"

Damn, he is one cold muthafucker. I sat there in silence because I didn't know where to go after that. He sure didn't have to worry about me asking him any more questions about his personal life.

Chapter 24

Clayton

Hugs and Kisses

Monica's love ballad "Love All Over Me" was playing on the speakers throughout my house. I knew it was too early to be playing that type of song, but it just made me feel good to know that the budding relationship that I was beginning was coming along quite nicely. I danced around the room in my boxers because I was that happy. It had been a long time since I felt like this. I had been in love before, but it didn't last long because of infidelity. I was younger then too. Neither of us was ready to be committed to anyone else besides ourselves. I feel like I was ready now. Ready for love.

What could one ask for in a potential mate? He was a handsome doctor that cares about the community and the people he treats. I was a professional in law enforcement and working my way up the ladder to the top. I got dressed in some of my finest clothes. I looked in the mirror and liked what I saw. All that was missing was the person to have on my arm. I exited my home and hopped into my car. I flipped the radio on and Jennifer Hudson's "Dressed Up in Love" came on. A smile instantly covered my face. I hope that this was a sign of things to come. I was still a bit nervous, though. This would be our second date, and we were meeting at his house. I had already put the address to his place in my GPS and had it playing in the Bluetooth in my ear with the music softly playing.

It was about a half-hour drive to his place. I pulled up to a house that looked like a minimansion. It was too big for one person. He was a doctor, but I wondered how one person could afford such a lavish place. But it dawned on me that I didn't know how much a doctor makes or how long he had this place. I was a bit jealous. I could see me moving in this place and making it a complete home. I could only hope to do so.

I got out of my car and walked up the well-manicured front yard to the door of the house. This door looked to be a solid dark brown wooden door with three glass panels that were about a foot long. It showcased the class and taste of the owner. The door opened, and Anthony stood in the doorway with a warm smile on his face. He was even better looking than I remembered him. He had on a nice lounging suit that showed off his slightly muscular body.

"Hey, you." He reached his arms out waiting for me to embrace him back. I wasn't the sensitive type, but as soon as I wrapped my arms around him, I felt right at home. We let go after a few seconds; then he stepped back and let me into his home . . . maybe *our* home soon.

There was soft jazz playing in the background as I looked around the very well decorated home. He had vintage-looking chairs and armoires in the large foyer as soon as we entered the house. It had a small cascading staircase flowing down the middle of a small second-floor landing. The theme was a burgundy and floral pattern. He had great taste.

"You like?" he asked as he watched me take in the scenery of his home.

"I love it. You have very good taste. In décor *and* men." The last part was a pun to see if he would bite.

"Yes to both of those." He smiled. "Well, let's make our way into the living room where I have some wine and cheese waiting for us to nibble on before we get into the main course."

"You lead the way," I said as I gently placed my hand around his waist, ushering him in front of me. I followed behind while getting a good view of his behind. It was nice and round like I loved. He had class when he walked. He didn't flaunt or anything like that. There was a natural flow to his walk.

We walked into a living room with very exquisite furniture. The furniture had wood moldings that lined the parameter of the front with feet that looked like that of an animal's foot. You could tell that this was not cheap furniture that was bought from Ikea. He probably had this stuff shipped from another country. A fireplace was blazing, but there was no heat coming from it. I looked at it in amazement.

"It's a state-of-the-art electronic fireplace. It's good for ambience in the warmer months and rolls up to reveal a live fireplace behind it," he enlightened me.

"This is absolutely top-notch. I think I'm in the wrong profession," I laughed.

"Well, I work hard for all of this."

"I bet you do. That's a Jewish hospital you work for. I'm glad to see that they are not cheap when it comes to the people that work for them."

"True." He nodded his head in agreement.

"You are not lacking either. I see the car that you drove up in. The city of Baltimore is not as deficient as they have led us to believe."

"Please, I am nowhere near where you are. I have a few more rungs on the ladder before I even come close to *this*." I waved my hand as if I was Vanna White showcasing a product.

"Well, let's move from pockets and dollars and get to really know each other." He changed the subject with agility and humor. "Have a seat on the sofa so we can really serve the tea."

"Well, what would you like to know?" I started off the question-and-answer phase of the date.

"Tell me, why did you become an officer of the law?" He rested his arm on the back of the couch and slightly turned toward me as he posed the question.

"It runs in the family. My father and grandfather were officers. So, it seemed the only logical choice to make. They are all retired now, so I am the lone gunman, as they say, in the family right now. What about you?"

"Well, no one in my family is as educated as I am. Not knocking them, though. I was very bright as a child in school. My teachers took a liking to me, and I was blessed to be pushed into my purpose. I now take care of my parents and my two younger siblings." He looked sexy as he talked. He had nice thick lips that gleamed some.

"What would you be doing if you could not be doing what you are doing now?" he asked. I had to admit that that was a very good question.

"I'd be a ho," I answered. He looked at me for a second and then burst into laughter. I loved his laugh as well. It was so freeing to hear. It was loud and boisterous. I couldn't help but laugh along with him.

"No, I really don't know. I've never thought about that. I love what I do. What about you?" I threw the question right back at him.

He paused for a few seconds. His eyes danced in his head momentarily while he thought. "Well, something in the medical field for sure. I love the human body and its form. God has blessed my hands. I smell our dinner finishing up. Let me go check on it. I'll be right back."

He got up from the sofa and walked out of the room. I wanted to scream in excitement as if I were a schoolgirl. It also gave me time to get my thoughts together and wonder what he might be asking next when he came back.

It didn't take him long to come back into the room with a glowing smile on his face. "Dinner is ready. Follow me to ecstasy." He turned and used his index finger over his shoulder to beckon me to follow him.

I rose from the sofa and followed behind him. The dining area was just as nice as the rest of the house. I could get used to this. I could be the house husband that he needed and deserved. I just needed to convince him of such.

He seated me, and then went back into his kitchen. A great aroma followed him as he made his way back into the room.

A meal of braised lamb and seasoned vegetables was presented perfectly. We said a quick prayer over the food and began to dig in. In between forkfuls of good food, we continued to talk.

"So, where do you see this going?" he asked. The question caught me off guard, but I was happy he was thinking about a future. Maybe I was in it. I wasn't in it for the money, but it was a good add-on to the package before me.

"I see a bright future and infinite possibilities." I hoped that was a good enough answer for him.

"That's nice to hear. I hope that it is going to happen. I have a very good feeling about you. Love is a necessity in this life."

"I believe that as well," I agreed.

We finished our food and the rest of the night went by without a problem. No physical intimacy happened, but the intangible intimacy was on point.

Chapter 25

Avery

Check In

"Hello," she answered the phone as if she was surprised to hear from me.

"Good day, Monica. I was calling to check up on you." I tried to sound convincing, but it was hard. Her tone of her voice told me that she needed something.

"Really?" There was some disbelief in her voice.

"Yes, I normally don't get personal with the parents of the children I rear, but I felt a connection to you. There is something about you that is enchanting."

"That's nice to hear."

"It was nice to say, and it is the truth. You will not get anything less than that from me." You must plant lies in the heads of others so they get a picture of you in their head that's not painted by themselves. I was a Picasso of minds. I painted you a picture of me long before you made up your mind about me.

"Now, that's nice to hear as well."

"So are you and your husband okay?" I moved on with my plans. I already knew the answer. I just wanted to hear it from her lips.

"Well, that didn't go exactly as planned."

"Wow, really? It seemed like a sure thing." I feigned hope and concern.

"Yes, I felt the same thing. Something is just off, and I don't know what to do."

"I don't know how to say this, but I will ask. Are you sure he's not with another woman?"

"My husband is not that type of man." She sounded convincing. She believed it. I did as well, but I still had to put it in her mind.

"Monica, no man is that dedicated. Men are creatures of habit. If habits change, then so does the creature."

"I don't believe that." She sounded defiant. I loved it.

"You don't have to believe the truth for it to be true. You just die because of your ignorance."

There was silence on her end of the phone. Maybe I hit her too hard with the last words that I gave her.

"Are you still there?"

"Yes, I'm here, or what's left of me," she chuckled after she spoke.

"The truth stings, but it can be rather healing in the end. Truth is I don't know what your husband is capable of. I just wanted to give you a different point of view."

"I appreciate that. It's what I needed to hear. It wasn't easy to hear but necessary."

"Well, I don't want to hold you. I was just checking in on my star player's mother."

"Again, I appreciate the call."

I hung up and smiled to myself. I was deep in my lair and work on plans to seal the deal on my hold of the city.

Chapter 26

Leroy

Making Amends

I was sitting in a meeting with my some of my leaders, and my mind was clouded with my family, mainly, my wife. I had to make it up to her. Maps and graphs were spread across the table, but all I could think about was my hand around my wife's neck in the shower the other day. I saw so much fear in her eyes in those few seconds. I was a man on the edge, and I needed to get my bearings before I lost it all.

"Y'all continue this shit and keep me posted on the progress. I have to take care of some things." I got up from my chair and exited one of my safe houses. It wasn't late, and I had to do something to make amends with my wife. There was no reason for my behavior over the last few weeks. And putting my hands on her was a no-no. I had to recover the situation. I can't let my kingdom rise and my castle fall. That would be stupid.

I knew what my wife liked, and those were the places I went to get some gifts to cater to her at this moment. Every woman loves pampering and surprises. I was going to blow her out of the water. I shopped to no end to satisfy myself and my wife. It's true what they say: "happy wife happy life." My wife has been there for me through it all, and I needed to acknowledge that. This was all my fault, and guilt was pushing me to get more, which I did. During the shopping, I texted my son to request that he get his mother out of the house for a few hours so that I could go home and set everything up. I knew that I had to make it up to him as well, but it wouldn't take much for me to get back in his good graces. I knew that my son wanted me at his practice and games, but he understood what a man had to do for his family. I made sure I trained him on providing for his family at all costs. I was sacrificing for the greater good of all our lives.

I got home and set up the house as best as I could get it in anticipation for my queen to arrive home. I talked to my son a few times while setting up, giving him instructions. His last instruction was to drop my wife off at home and make up an excuse to go out with friends.

The jingling of keys in the door signaled my wife's arrival back home. As soon as she entered the house, she was greeted with a huge bouquet of white and yellow roses. Her face was full of surprise. I loved it.

"What's this for?" she inquired, stunned.

"This is sorry for all that has happened over the last few weeks. My queen, you are my world, and I don't want you to forget."

"Roy, I'm speechless." She covered her mouth with her hand. A few tears slipped down her face letting me know that she was getting emotional and in a good way. I knew I was at the threshold of forgiveness.

"It's not over. Let's go into the living room. There's more," I said as I gently guided her with my hands around her waist. I was excited to see the look on her face when she got there.

We got to the room, and her face lit up once again.

"This is . . ." She couldn't even finish her statement because she was looking at a brand-new living-room set that I had to pay big bucks to get here on such short notice. On the sofa was all kinds of pocketbooks, shoes, and outfits that I knew she would adore. I did pay attention to my wife's taste a lot of the time because if I hadn't, I would have been in trouble trying to put this together and making sure she would approve. My phone vibrated letting me know that her other gift had arrived and was at the front of the house waiting. I knew that she would love this.

"Monica, it's not over. Go to the front door and open it, please."

"What have you done?" She smiled. She was almost giddy with excitement.

I trailed behind her as she went to the front door and opened it.

"Oh my Lord!" She covered her mouth with both her hands in sheer joy.

"Is it mine?" she asked.

"Yes, take him or her."

She reached her hands out and pulled the Yorkipoo dog out of the hands of a dog farmer whom I also lucked out and got to come all this way from close to D.C. to get the dog here. My wife has always wanted to have one of these, but I was a no-pet type of guy. I had to show her that I was serious about how sorry I was. If this wasn't enough, then I don't know what else I could do.

She came back in the house, and I closed the door behind us, but not before I handed off three stacks to get that damn shit factory here on such short notice.

My wife was all over that dog. Shit, she forgot I was even in the room now.

"You like him?" I asked, more so to get some attention back on me.

"Leroy, you have totally outdone yourself. I'm just floored by all of this."

"Nothing is too much for you, baby. Nothing." I smiled and secretly patted myself on the back. I was just hoping that this was enough to keep her occupied and busy. I was going to continue to be absent for as long as it took to get my empire where I wanted it to be. This ghost guy was not making it easy to track him down, but I was determined, and I would not stop until he was at my feet.

Chapter 27

Monica

Smoke Screen

I sat on my new living-room set still in awe. "Leroy, you really did it up," I said to myself out loud. It was a few days after he lavished me with tons of gifts and my new Yorkipoo dog.

"What is this all about?" I raised Monroe, that's what I named the dog Leroy gave me, into the air and talked to him. The conversation that I had with Coach the other day was still in the back of my mind. My husband was saying he was sorry for mistreating me, but was this all that it was about? I mean, my husband knew my sizes and all when it came to dresses and bras, which is rare for a husband, especially one that was in the street life. It made me wonder who helped him with all of this. He couldn't have done all of this by himself. Could he?

"I just don't know what to think any more. So much has changed over time, and I'm totally lost in a marriage that I was completely sure of a few short months ago. Now, I don't know if these gifts were an apology for something else and how he was treating me or just how he was neglecting me.

"What do you think, Monroe?" The dog looked at me, but nothing came out, which was expected. I didn't want to become one of the CSI wives, but I think I just may have to do some detective work and see what else has my husband's attention out in the streets.

I needed some help in that area because I have never had any reason to do it. I need someone who is impartial in the matter and has nothing to gain from it.

Today was one of the last days of practice before the boys' basketball team started their city tournament, and I was going to have to pull Coach aside and ask him if he knew someone who could do a little spy work for me.

"Ma, you ready to go?" Corey yelled as he came down the steps. He seemed more upbeat these last few days. I guess the anger that he had when I told him about his father was dissipating over time.

"Yeah, Corey. I have to get the dog carrier; then we can be on our way."

"Ma, can you do me a favor and don't ever refer to that dog as a sibling of mine." He looked serious.

"Boy, go ahead out to the car and get out of my face. Besides, your little brother's feelings is hurt by that. Just look at his face." I held Monroe up to him and then laughed. Corey smirked but then left the room for the car. I did what I said and was in the car in minutes.

"Corey, so why are you so happy all of a sudden?" I asked as I hopped on the expressway.

"What do you mean, Ma? I'm always happy."

"You weren't happy when I told you about your father the other day, so that actually cancels the word 'always,' son."

He looked at me like I had said something wrong. "Ma, that is not the same. That was an isolated situation. I'm over that now."

"I can see that. I think there's a person in your life that is fueling this happiness. Am I correct?"

"Why does it have to be a person to make me happy? I can't be happy on my own?" He had an attitude.

"Corey, that didn't answer my question. You're avoiding it. Good job with the evasive offensive defense. I'm not the one, though. Answer my question."

"Ma, I'm a single man. I'm happy of my own accord."

"She better be treating you right. That's all I'm saying."

He didn't say anything after that because he knew that I was aware of the change of pattern. He was a happy guy. But today, he was just floating almost. I remember that feeling all too well in the beginning stages of his father's and my relationship. I still loved his father. I just wasn't "floating" at the moment.

It didn't take long before we were pulling up at the gymnasium. I exited the car, and Corey grabbed his gear out of the backseat. I was glad to see my son at practice most days, but today was all about me. I couldn't wait to pull Coach to the side and see if he knew anyone that could help me. I had a strong feeling that he knew someone.

Practice seemed like it was taking forever to end, and when it finally did, I was down those bleachers and headed over to where the coach was standing.

"Coach, may I have a moment of your time?" I asked after all the boys went into the shower area.

"Sure, is everything okay?"

"Yes and no. I need you ask you something in your office. It's rather personal."

"Sure, follow me this way."

I followed him, and as soon as we both sat down and got settled, he looked at me and waited for me to begin.

"Well, after the incident with my husband, he decided that he would surprise me with a few lavish gifts that were all on point in every way imaginable. But it also made me curious as to the motives."

"Motives?" he questioned.

"Yes, motives. I don't know if my husband is sorry or cheating. I have never been worried about my husband until he picked out clothes and bras in my size precisely. I think some chick is helping him or trying to get at him. I hope not, but that's what I feel."

"Feelings don't have facts, Monica. They never do. With that being said, what do you need from me?"

"Well, I'm hoping that you had a friend or someone that can spy on my husband. He's not an easy target, but I can give you some information on places he frequents."

"I'm not sure about this, Monica. Is this *really* something that you want to do?" His hands were folded on the desk in front of me. He looked concerned.

"Yes, I just want to put this feeling to rest."

"Okay, well, I have a friend that I can call; then I can report any findings to you. I hope and pray that he finds nothing. You are a nice lady, and your husband is probably just busy. You don't just develop these problems; they are there from the beginning. If you say he wasn't like that in the beginning, then he probably hasn't changed, but I will do what you ask and since your son is my star player, I'll do this on the house. He owes me a favor anyway."

"Thanks, Coach, and please leave my son out of this. He doesn't need to know anything until I'm sure of the situation."

"I can respect that." He nodded his head in agreement.

I reached out and shook his hand, and then exited his office. Coach seemed more confident about my husband than I did . . . and that worried me.

Chapter 28

Corey

Perks

"That's it right there." I had my hand on the back of Dre's head as he bobbed up and down on my manhood. The feeling of power over a person can be quite exhilarating. I see why my father was trying to do what he was trying to do in the streets. Being at the top had some very great perks. Yes, I was still a bit apprehensive when it came to Dre because he had my secret, but that was still on the back burner of my cares. Dre was looser than he was when it came to being sexually free from the first time in the motel. He was the perk of my father being his boss and of my father's disdain for the homosexual movement.

Money, power, and sex . . . They reigned well together, and I was loving it. I didn't have the money per se, because it was my father's, but I did share in it, for sure. I was just beginning to get the taste for power, and you already know where I am with sex.

We've been at the hotel for about fifteen minutes, and this is where he started . . . on his knees. For a guy that was as well built as he was, he sure was submissive, and I could get used to it. I had two other boys that I would knock off from time to time, but they just may have met their match. I wasn't in love or any of that, but this guy was mature and handled himself like a pro. Maybe mature men are the way to go. Now, he was not senile or old. He had me by at least ten years. It's said age is nothing but a number, but we'll see. I hope that this dude is loyal. He got my life in his hands for sure. I didn't want my business out in the streets, and I hope he don't try no ransom type of shit with my secret. He didn't seem like the dumb type, but we have only been in contact with each other twice. I want to see what he's all about and how he hid his sexuality from my father. I could see, but I wanted to pick his mind.

"Dre, get up for a minute," I requested. He looked at me with confusion on his face. I'm sure he has never been told to stop giving head, but I wanted talk first. I should have started with this, though, then with the head, but this question shit didn't hit me until now when I was getting some head from him.

"Something wrong?" he asked. I had to admit he was a handsome guy. I'm sure the ladies were all over him.

"Nah, I just wanted to ask you some things."

"Cool." He wasn't a man of many words when it came to us interacting during sex. He sat in a chair that was in front of the bed we were on with his hands in his lap. You couldn't tell that he just had his mouth on my manhood. This guy was good. He had his shit covered.

"Man, how do you do it?" I asked.

"Do what?"

"Man, my father is a hardcore homophobe. He's like a savage pit bull waiting to take this ghost guy down, and here he has a gay guy working right under his nose. How do you feel about that?"

"Your father has a right to feel like he feels. I can't change that." He was just so plain with his talk, and he showed no emotion.

"So you saying it doesn't bother you when he calls gay men derogatory names?"

"Nah, it's what you answer to, not what you're called. He wasn't talking about me or to me. I know who I am." He gave up a Tyler Perry response, but I can agree with it.

"So you don't want to beat my father's ass sometimes?" I laughed.

"Nope, been in this business for a while now, and I have heard it all in the streets. People say and do what they want to with no regard to others, and that's how they live. I mind my business and keep it home."

"Dre, you are cool as shit, man. So why do you let me hold you hostage with your secret?"

"It's temporary. Most gay men get tired of the same hole, so they most definitely move on rather quickly. I've been there and done that too. You're going to get tired of me and move on, so I'll just wait until such a time." Damn, he was spitting the truth to me. You could tell he believed it and lived it too.

"Dre, I really don't know if all of that's true, but I am convinced that you have some experience in, so I'm going to take you at your word."

"What else do I have besides my words?"

This ninja was on point. I laughed in my head but kept a straight face.

"That is true. So how did you get into the drug game?"

"It's a family thing like yours, with the exception that my older brothers didn't make it. They weren't cut out for it. They had too much mouth and didn't know how to chill. They balled out, as they say, and got taken out in the middle of it. Your pops don't unnecessarily flaunt his. I been with him for a minute now, and I know how to conduct myself, especially with someone else's business. He helped me refine my attitude, and now I'm the man you see."

"So are there any other guys on the DL in my father's camp?"

"I don't fucking care or ask. I said I keep my shit home. I don't care about anyone else's sex life." He said it as if I was getting on his nerves or he was offended.

"I got you, dude. No need to jump down my throat." I laughed, hoping that it would lighten the mood.

"I'm not offended at all. Life is too short to hold on to offense. I just wanted to make it clear where I stand." He smiled.

"So I take it that I can trust you with my secret, and yours is safe with me."

He nodded his head in agreement.

"So now that that's out of the way let me get in them guts."

Chapter 29

Clayton

Bàn tài

Here I am trying to focus on this case, and all I can do is think about Anthony. Fresh love can be very distracting at times. Today was one of those times. I was sitting at my desk looking over some evidence and files but could not keep my focus.

I had most of my focus on Ghost right now because he was the leading man in my eyes, but he wasn't the only man. There was another man in my scope. I had my eyes on Leroy Grant, but he was good at his game too. I knew that he was guilty, but he had never been caught with his hands dirty. He had a somewhat clean record. We knew that he would slip up one day, and we were waiting for that day. There have been some turf wars going on between the gay thugs and the straight ones. Murders were happening almost daily, but it never seemed like it slowed down the business of drug traffic and other illicit activities. Taking down evil was hard because there is always someone ready, willing, and able to take the spot of the last kingpin. Now we had two men warring: one to continue to stay on top and the other trying to dethrone him. It was mind-boggling, to say the least. So, I mentally decided to go after the gay thugs. In my mind, they would be the most rewarding to take down. The straight thugs will kill themselves off or get caught easier. It's just my logic, though. Things could change at the drop of a dime, and I end up getting both leaders in my grasp. They say the thrill of the chase is what keeps you going, and I had to agree. I was going to get my man and have a budding relationship to boot. It was a dream come true. Everything was falling into place.

It made me think back to when I was a teenager. I would always look at my parents and see them enjoying their life. They seemed perfect to me. I never saw them fight or any of that. My father would work, and my mom would work part time. He was a cop, and she did day care. They made it work, and I was so looking forward to that type of happiness. I couldn't wait to be that happy. Both of my parents would be happy for me if they were here today. Tragically, they died in a car accident that killed them on the spot. It was the most tragic moment in my life. So, you can say that my life and living was dedicated to them. A drug dealer running from the police took their life, and I promised them at their funeral that I would make it my life's work to keep killers off the streets.

I sat in the back of the funeral parlor just looking at the two caskets that were located at the front of the room. It was cold in the room. One would say that it was beautiful in this room. Flowers filled the front with large pictures of my parents on easels. I was cold. I cut my emotions off because I didn't want to grieve. I didn't want to believe this reality, even though I was sitting in this room, and there were two bodies that were present that used to be my parents. They were empty shells now.

Dozens of people came past me to view the bodies, and they tried to console me. My parents were pillars in their community. I wasn't accepting the consoling. I was in pain. I was mad at God for allowing this to happen to them and to me. I was mad at him for letting the scum that did this to them live. I was only here because this is what they would want me to do. To be here like they were there for me regardless of the situation. Their examples of doing what is right is present in my life. Principles, morals, and compassion were a part of their living and now mine.

The service began as normal, and I tried to keep my focus on what was going on, but my mind was on the killer that violated my life. I wanted him and all who were like him to pay. That was my vow.

At the close of the service, they called for the last viewing of the bodies. I rose from the chair, but I felt like I was moving in slow motion as I got closer to my destination. My legs became weaker with every step, and by the time I made it to the front, I fell to my knees with a hand on the end of one casket and beginning of the other one. I bellowed out loud cries of pain, and tears fell like heavy rain. I felt my body being lifted, and then being hoisted up by fellow mourners.

"They will pay . . . they will pay . . . they will pay," I hollered out in front of everyone in the room until exhaustion caused me to stop.

Their legacy and death was my reason for living. I wanted them to look down from heaven and smile. I'm not sure if they knew about me being gay and all, but I'm sure that they would be proud of me, nonetheless. I am going to make history by bringing down at least one of these guys, and I could not wait for it to happen. I was falling in love with my dreams every day.

As I was looking through some of the pictures of the body that I looked at the other day, I noticed a tattooed symbol in the inner thigh of the victim's body. It looked like some kind of Asian mark or something. I used an app on my phone to scan the picture. It took a few seconds to come back with results.

The symbol in Chinese meant *Biàn tài* or "Metamorphosis" in English. It made sense with the transition the body I saw went through. I just had to see if there was any type of coincidence or trademark. Any type of clue to finding out who was doing these changes to these people would lead back to the financier of the operations. Somebody was getting paid to do this, and one would lead to the other.

I placed a call to the city morgue again and asked to get any more pictures of bodies that had this symbol. I requested they be sent to me if they found some.

A smile covered my face as I hung up the phone. I felt like I was making progress and that I was on my way to something big.

Chapter 30

Avery

Photo Op

I was a person of many talents but being a photographer was not my forte. I had money so that I could pay someone to do it for me. I knew my limits. I had expectations of the pictures that I wanted, but what I received a few hours ago from the private investigator that I hired to get these photos for me was an expert. He had some great shots in the bunch that I had. I had so many that my graphic designer could work with. I was excited.

I know you may be wondering, why not kill the competition if I knew where they lay their head, or why not send the cops their way to put them away forever? Well, it's just not fun to do that. That would be too easy. I loved to be entertained, and this was one of the best shows that I could ever watch and participate in. It was the real-deal reality television show, but there were no cameras, and I was the director of the show, and I had a starring role in it as well.

I picked up the phone and called a person who was waiting on me to call.

"Hello," Monica answered the phone on what seemed like the first ring.

"Good day, Monica. How is everything with you today?" It was a Saturday.

"I'm doing wonderful," she answered. I wanted to burst her bubble and tell her that she was lying and that she was on pins and needles waiting for the truth to fall in her lap, whatever that may be. But that wasn't going to be done. She needed some comfort before the blow. I didn't know how she would respond by finding out that her husband was cheating on her.

"That's so good to hear. I was hoping that your day and week was going well. You didn't stick around for the last few practices with Corey, and I began to get worried." I was baiting her, and I loved it.

"Coach, I apologize for that. I had some errands I needed to run, and I couldn't do both. You know how it gets sometimes. Besides, Corey understood."

"Yes, he passed the message on to me when I asked about your whereabouts. I was concerned because of the previous conversation we had and the favor you asked of me. I know it was not something easy to ask of a person. It took some nerve for me to call because I didn't want to be insensitive to your state of mind."

"Coach, I'm glad you called because I wanted to call you as well. I am so glad that you considered my feelings, though. That is an honorable thing to do."

"No problem." I paused. "I was actually calling to let you know that my friend would be delivering the evidence you requested very soon. I'm praying for the positive. I don't think you have a thing to worry about, however. From what you tell me, your husband seems like a very stand-up guy."

"It seems like you have more faith than I do now," she stated.

"That's not hard to believe. Doubt will do that to you."

"Yes, that is true. I just want things to go back to the way they were before. Do you know someone with a damn time machine or something?" she joked.

I laughed, and then spoke, "Monica that is something all of us would want to use. But, no, I don't know anyone with one of those. And I don't know if I would share the information if I did." I laughed after I talked, hoping that she would as well. She did.

"Monica, I won't hold you. I was just calling to let you know the progress of your request."

"Thanks for the call."

"I'll talk to you soon or see you even sooner. Have a great day." I hung up the phone, sat back in my chair, and smiled. I was a bad muthafucker.

Chapter 31

Leroy

Good Vibes

Happy wife, happy wife, I thought to myself as I sat at the kitchen table.

I smiled on the inside because I was seeing the fruits of my labor. My wife walked around the kitchen humming as she did usually when she was happy and life was good. I'm glad that the gifts that I bought her had calmed her down and made her more chipper than before the gift giving. I'm going to have to follow up with some other things soon because I don't want her to think that it's just to keep her quiet. I loved my wife, and as soon as I get this drug game on lock, we're heading off on a trip to Europe. It's always been a dream of hers, and I'm going to give it to her. She deserves the best, and I will stop at nothing to get it for her. It was one of the main reasons for chasing this so hard. My wife looks at me as her king and expects the best, and if I can't get the city from a gay man, then what does that make me look like? A man who is not respected in his house first doesn't have it anywhere else.

"Monica, you are looking extrafly today," I said getting up from the table and walking up to her as she washed some dishes. I nestled up behind her and put my hands around her waist and squeezed her tight. I put my nose in between her head and shoulder area and breathed in her scent. I almost forgot how good my lady smelled. I've been going hard in the game to forget her scent.

"Thank you, baby." Her voice was sweet and seductive. It made my manhood hard. I hadn't sexed my wife in a minute, and I needed to feel her right now. I was pressed for time, but I wanted her right now.

"Baby, come with me for a minute," I requested as I moved away from her and pulled her away from the sink.

"What's wrong, baby?" she asked as I pulled her into the first-floor bathroom.

"Nothing, baby. I just wanted some quality time really quick." A sly smile crept across my face. I locked the door and turned on the sink water to muffle some of the sounds. My son was still in the house. He was probably asleep, but I didn't want him to hear me sexing his mother at any age.

Monica had on a robe that was to her knees. I aggressively turned her around and grinded my manhood into her behind. She moaned a little as my hands made their way up the sides of her waist, up her abdomen, and finally to her breasts. I teased her now-erect nipples in between two of my fingers, and she grinded her behind into my lap harder.

I pulled away and then lifted the robe over her waist. I eased down her underwear, and then dived in with my tongue. She was already wet. It had been a minute since I lapped at her vagina, but it was much needed right now. The stress of the drug game was taking its toll on me.

I immediately went into dog mode. I was like a dehydrated dog at the water bowl. She pushed back on my face causing me to fall back on the floor. That didn't stop us, though. She was soon straddling my face and was working my manhood out of my zippered pants and into her mouth. The warmth of her mouth led me to work even harder at getting her to cream on my face. It didn't take long for her to start shaking and then exploding on my face.

"Damn," she quivered in ecstasy.

"My turn," I said as I eased her off me, and then positioned her on all fours in front of me. I entered her slowly and savored the moment. I hadn't exploded in a long time. Again, the drug game and the obsession to be on top will even drain a man's sex drive.

She clutched one of my hands that was on her waist as I entered her fully. She was enjoying it. I was too. I couldn't believe how tight my wife's pussy was. She was a faithful wife, and I loved it.

I started with a slow pace, but soon, I was moving in and out of her at a good pace. I went from doggie style to froggy style as I hovered over her. I nibbled on her ear and whispered in it, "Damn, girl, this shit is tight and wet. I love you, girl."

She moaned in response to my statement, and that was enough for me. I pumped in and out of her feverishly; then I climaxed. I came so hard that I roared in pleasure. I hoped that my son didn't hear us, but at this point, I didn't care.

"Baby, that was the shit. We need to do this more often," I said as I eased off her and lay on the floor next to her.

"True," she nodded her head in agreement.

"I need to shower again and get out of here," I said as I kissed her on the cheek. I quickly got up and made my way out of the bathroom. I climbed the stairs to get to the bathroom in my room. My son was coming out of his bathroom as I was walking.

"Good morning," I smiled at my boy. He was a grown man coming into his own. He looked like me at his age. It was almost time to bring him into the fold and teach him about the business. He must be prepared if something happens to me.

"Hey, Dad," he said as he kept it moving past me and back into his bedroom. I was going to have to spend some time with him again soon too. I don't want him to think that he wasn't important either. There were some rough patches between us over the last few weeks, but I'm sure we'll work them out. I hope he wasn't still mad at me for the incident with his mother awhile back. Corey was very protective of his mother, and I was no exception on his list of people he would hurt if anything happened to her. It shows me that he had heart and courage. He would take a life for his mother, even if it was mine. That would never happen, however, because those were isolated incidents, and he knew that.

I showered and changed my clothes, and then made my way out of the house. I had good vibes going on and getting the ups on this ghost guy was in those vibes. I was so close I could smell the come-up.

Chapter 32

Monica

Pleased or Please!

Some good dick isn't going to give me amnesia, even if it was from my husband. But I had to admit that it was damn good dick. That nut he gave me made me weak. I had to lie there for a minute to get myself together. But in the back of my mind, all the suspicions and questions were still there. I gave up the goods because, frankly, I wanted to come.

Every wife wants to spend time with their husband. The problem with tons of men is that they'd rather buy us things or come in us to make us feel appreciated, when most of the time all we wanted was time spent. Watch a television show or movie with us, even if you don't like it. Go with us shopping and help us pick out a few things. Don't just give us the plastic and send us on our way. It will all be in vain. And soon, we'll turn to someone else or plastic for pleasure.

I've been trying to keep myself busy for weeks with things around the house after he left, but I couldn't keep my mind away from my own wandering thoughts. I even went to the bookstore to get some books so that it could take me away from my reality. I was driving myself crazy being inside of my own head. All the conversations I was having with myself were driving me crazy. Thank

God Corey had his first game in a couple of hours. It will be a welcomed outing, for sure. I was so proud of how ambitious my son was. He was very much like his father. I just hoped that he didn't have *all* his traits, mainly, the slackness of attention for his mate.

"Hey, Ma, you ready to go?" My handsome son came into my bedroom as I was lying across the bed with a book in my hand, but I wasn't focused on it.

"Yes," I replied, and then slid off the bed like I was too sluggish to move.

"Dang, Ma, you sure you're ready?" he let out a slight laugh.

"Yes, why do you ask that?"

"Because of the way you slid out of the bed just now."

"I'm just into this book. It's so good, I didn't want to put it down." I put on a faint smile to try to divert the conversation and my true feelings. I was hurting on the inside.

"You sure it's not old age or something?" He covered his mouth with his hand to stifle a laugh, but it didn't work. It did cause me to laugh too, though. My son always had a way of getting you all the way together. He was my anchor, and he didn't even know it.

"Give me a minute to get dressed," I said.

"Cool, just don't take forever. This is my first game, and I'm going to show out. I don't want Coach all over me because you want to look extrafabulous or something," he said as he stood by the door.

"Boy, get out of here and wait downstairs. We'll be on time," I said as I picked up a slipper and threw it at him.

It took me about twenty minutes to get ready, and I was looking fabulous, I might add.

I drove like a bat out of hell getting to the gymnasium. As soon as we got there, Corey hopped out of the car and sprinted toward the door. He was amped up and ready to go. I was so proud of him.

As soon as I got out of the car, I received the shock of my life.

"Hey, baby. I know you're surprised to see me, but you don't have to look like you saw a ghost." My husband walked up to me with one of his men with him. He pulled me into his body with both his arms and kissed me on the lips. I had to admit that I *was* shocked. He didn't say that he was coming to the game. He didn't say he wasn't either. I loved my husband, and the fact that he was here was great. It just felt like he was a different person than when I married him. His obsession was changing him and me. I didn't like it. I like when I had control of my family. Maybe that control was an illusion that is only now being revealed.

Chapter 33

Corey

Game On

We came out of the locker room blazing fast. I was in the back because a good leader doesn't go first; he goes last. The stands were crowded with parents and supporters. It felt good to be all hyped and ready to rumble. We all gathered on the side and huddled with the coach. He gave us a rousing speech like he just did in the locker room. He smiled this time, though. I knew he was ready for a win. He was expecting it. He pushed us out to the floor, and we aligned ourselves to our respective positions. I looked around at the atmosphere of the gym. At least 200 people were packed into this place. I looked at the smiling faces and the handwritten signs that were being displayed on both sides of the court. I lived for these moments. I was in my element, and I wasn't going to disappoint the people in the building. They came for a good game, and I was going to give them one.

My heart was racing, and I sized my opponent up quickly. He was a tall guy with some muscle on him. He had tattoos going down both of his arms that stopped at his elbows. His dreaded-up hair hung just past his ears. He was a handsome guy in my opinion. He had fire in his eyes, and he came to win.

So did I.

I was like the lion in the jungle getting ready to go in for the kill. Then, out of nowhere, I heard a voice that I wasn't ready for but knew all too well.

"Go, Corey!" I looked around to see if it was true. It was my father in the stands. He didn't say anything about coming, but he was here. He was nestling up against my mother. She had an uncomfortable look on her face; then I spotted Dre next to my father. I was more excited to see Dre than I was my father. Did that say something about our relationship? Probably did, but in these few seconds, I didn't care because the referee blew the whistle and threw the ball in the air. I grabbed it out of the air and went for the goal. I hit the three-point line and sank in a three-pointer. The people in the bleachers went wild. The smile on my coach's face was rewarding. I looked up into the stands and saw my father smiling, but it didn't mean as much to me.

The game pretty much went the way we wanted it to go. We dominated and dismantled the opposing team. The score was 54–33, our win. I was superexcited to be the lead player and a winner. It was a highlight of my life.

After all the hoopla died down in the locker room, my father and mother met me outside. I had to admit that I was tired after all the moves I pulled off on the court.

I walked of the gym doors and was greeted by my family standing at the car waiting for me. It felt good to have a support system in place. Talking to many of the guys I played with let me know that I was blessed because many only had one parent in their lives. I was fortunate to have both. My father wore a look of admiration and pride. My mother did as well. I was so glad to have a family, even if we weren't the "normal" type of family.

"Son, you were hot out there tonight. You are a true beast." My father gave me a pound and then grabbed me into a manly hug.

My mother followed with a hug; then Dre and I just nodded our heads with a "what's up?" I lusted after him in my mind. And the way he took small glances at me let me know he felt the same. He looked hot standing next to my father in a suit and tie. He took his role in my father's mob seriously. I was learning to respect him even more as the days went by. I couldn't help visualizing him taking my dick either. That would make my night. I could and would muster up the energy to get a nut out tonight if we could get away.

Before we could do anything else, Coach came out of the doors and walked up to us.

"Great job, Corey," he said as he patted me on the shoulder.

"Coach, this is my father, Leroy."

"Leroy, you did a great job training this boy. He's going to go far in life." He reached out to shake my father's hand. They shook; then Coach went on his way.

"Babe, I'm taking my boy out for a celebration. I'ma meet you back home later to finish what we started the other day." He hit her on butt and then smiled.

"So, I don't get to celebrate with my son too?" She put her hand on her hip and looked at me, and then him.

"Babe, next time. I promise that I got you, and we'll do it as a family on the next win." He grabbed her hand, and then pulled her closer to him. He gave her a peck on the cheek and then released her. She looked at me with disappointment, but I didn't want to start any drama, so I just agreed.

"Yeah, Ma. We got you next time." I kissed her on the cheek too. The look in her eye was one of hurt, but I didn't know what else to do or say. I didn't want to go, but my dad was trying to mend broken fences, and it was only right to try on my end as well.

I think my parents are back on track anyway. I remember coming downstairs the other day and her coming out of the bathroom with a sly smile on her face, but as soon as she looked at me, she looked away. I knew that my parents were getting it in from time to time. I just thank God that I have never walked in on it or heard it. She turned and walked to her car; then we did the same thing.

We ended up doing the same thing we did every time my father wanted to celebrate or relax.

The strip club.

Titties, ass, money, and liquor flowed freely. It didn't take long for the ladies to flock their way in our direction. My father was well known, and especially in places like this. More than half of these people were funding our family's lives. My father had his hand in the drug game, but he also had a stake in a few clubs. He wanted to make sure we had more than what we needed, and that it stayed that way. I respected that.

I had to put on a better show than the ladies that were throwing their bodies in front of us. My smile and jubilee matched that of my father and Dre's. I knew for a fact that Dre and I were not the least bit interested in any of these ladies. Dre didn't get in too deep with the activities because he was my father's security, along with a few other guys sprinkled around the room. My eyes zeroed in on Dre and his interaction with the ladies that were throwing their ass all over him. He played the role of a straight hustler by smacking their asses, throwing money at them, and feeling their bodies up. He smiled in my direction, letting me know that he was thinking of me the whole time. I was doing the same things. If my father could read minds, we'd both be in trouble.

It didn't take long for me to become completely bored and lose interest in the activities. After the last chick left, I pulled out my phone and surfed Facebook.

"Son, don't tell me you ready to go. You can't let your old man outlast you." He leaned over to talk to me while a chick was grinding on his lap like she was trying to make the material disappear with her ass. She was undeniably putting in work. My father stuffed a twenty in her G-string, and then pushed her away.

"Dad, I'm just a bit tired from the game. It took a lot out of me, and I just want to lie down and get ready for practice again tomorrow. You know, practice makes perfect. I want nothing but the best, and that takes rest and dedication."

"Son, I admire that attitude. Let's get the hell out of here." He got up and made his way to the door. Dre was in front of us, and I looked back to see about six other guys follow suit.

Dre dropped us off at the house.

"Dad, I need Dre to go with me to the store really quick, and then bring me back. I want something to snack on."

"Do you, son? You have one of my right-hand men with you, so I know that you're good."

We pulled off and then dipped off to a spot that we were sure that no one would say or see a thing. It didn't take long for us to work out some sexual frustration, and this time, I let him take the lead, and we switched roles. I can't say it was an easy experience, but it was a pleasurable one indeed. I think I was falling for this dude. Shit. That was not in the plans at all.

"Dre, where is this going?" I asked. I didn't want to seem like the nagging type or girly, so I kept my face forward. I did want to know if he was feeling the same way or close, though. We were lying back in the seats that were reclined for our sex session.

"What do you mean?" he asked.

"I mean, are we labeling what we're doing?" It felt strange asking this because I have never had a labeled relationship. I messed around with a few people over time, but it was just sex and exploration to me. It felt like Dre and I had some relating going on.

"You cool with me, and I'm cool with you. No labels needed. I got your back, and you have mine. It's just that simple. It's between us and no one else. Feel me?" His hand made its way over to my thigh, and he rested it there. There was no more conversation needed. We had each other. Simple as that.

Chapter 34

Clayton

Surprise

My mind had been racing for quite some time about this case and these kingpins running amuck throughout the city. I just wanted a break. So when Anthony called me and invited me out on a day date, I was all too happy to accept his invitation.

I was at my desk working when my phone rang. My face lit up when I saw who it was.

"Heyyy." I was full of excitement. I loved the newness in my life called Anthony. He was a welcomed distraction for my daily grind.

"You working hard?" His voice sounded so sweet and loving. I could get used to it.

"I'm doing what I do well," I answered.

"I bet you are, handsome." It felt good to have someone to call me and gush on me.

"Thank you for the compliment."

"It's the truth, and that's part of the reason why I'm calling you. I wanted to see if you were available to go out on a day date."

"Hmmm . . . a day date? I wonder if I'm available." I played as if I was pondering the question.

"Don't wonder *too* long," he laughed.

"Just tell me when and where and I'll be there." A smile covered my face after my answer. I was giddy.

"I'll text you the information. See you then, my fine sir."

"I sure will." I hung up the phone and leaned back in my chair as I thought of all the possibilities of where Anthony and I were heading, relationship-wise.

I got off work early Friday just so I could go shopping and get me something special to wear. I didn't want to go out and be looking busted, not that I do that during the rest of the week. I just wanted to look special because I was feeling special.

Now it was Saturday, and I was dressed and ready to leave. I was especially glad that the sun was shining and there was a slight breeze blowing. I hopped into my car and turned my satellite radio on to the jazz station as I drove. I felt good. I felt *damn* good. I could see Anthony's face as I drove, and it made me smile. I couldn't believe that I was feeling this way right now. I was almost floating. I pulled into the quaint little spot in Canton that Anthony texted to me earlier that morning and was ready to go. I didn't know what we were going to talk about or what was going to happen, but I was excited.

As soon as I parked the car, I checked the rearview mirror to see if I looked presentable. When I was satisfied with my look, I got out of the car and walked toward the entrance of the establishment. It felt very comfortable and upscale as I made my way inside. There was an array of potted plants that lined the walk up to the door and had clinging plants that clung around the windowpanes. It had a small gated section with cast-iron chairs and linen-covered tables for eating outside.

"Hello, Mr. Clayton, your party is waiting for you," the maître d' smiled after he spoke. I looked at him in surprise because he knew my name and what I looked like, but I followed behind him when he turned and started walking.

It wasn't a huge restaurant so I could see Anthony sitting at the table with two other people. One man and one woman, visibly older but not feeble or frail. She was a bit plump, and he was on the thin side. They both had some grey in their hair. She was very beautiful, and the guy could get the dick if he swung that way. I immediately began to wonder what was going on. The investigative me began to try to decipher the situation before I got to the table, but I couldn't, so I just smiled as I arrived there.

"Clayton, babe, I'm so glad you could make it." He stood up and gave me a kiss on the lips. I was taken aback a bit because I didn't know who the people were at the table with him. I wanted and needed to know. I didn't feel comfortable not knowing who they were.

"Clayton, these are my parents, Sylvia and Graham Moore."

I was even more shocked than before. Parents? His parents? What in the hell?

"Hi, Anthony, Clayton has told us so much about you. We're so happy for you two." The mother got up and shook my hand. The father just looked at me, like I was a guy trying to take advantage of his daughter or something.

"Why, thank you. I'm so glad to meet you." I spoke with a smile plastered across my face like I was the Joker from *Batman*. My mind was swirling tremendously. This was a big step in any relationship. Meeting the parents. Who in the hell does this? I felt like I was being thrown under the bus. But I kept up the charade to save face. I could handle this situation. I've seen dead bodies and decomposition to great magnitudes. I could handle a surprise meeting of Anthony's parents. I was up for the challenge.

We all sat back down after a few more pleasantries; then I spoke. "This is such a wonderful surprise, Anthony."

"I thought that you would like it. I thought it was time." There is no official handbook on dating and meeting the parents of a love interest, but I'm sure that meeting the parents was quite some ways off in the dating process. If I'm not mistaken, it's closer to the marriage part of a relationship. We've only been dating a few weeks, so I didn't know what he was thinking, but I would ride with it for now. I haven't been in the dating pool in quite some time, and things probably have changed. I just hated being the odd man out.

"This was great timing," I lied.

"Yes, Clayton, we were surprised too, because Tony has not ever introduced us to anyone that he has ever been involved with until you. You must be special for all of us to be sitting here together." His father spoke so politely and well-mannered. He looked like he was proud of his son. It made my tension go down some.

"Yes, and to find out that you both would be getting married was an even bigger shock to us too," his mother said as she looked at me with glee-filled eyes.

My heart felt like it fell into my stomach. I looked at Anthony with a smile on his face. I had a "what the fuck!" on the edge of my tongue, but I swallowed it before I spoke.

"Yes, it was a surprise to me too. But your son is so special to me that I just couldn't hold back and let someone else snatch him up. Life is too short to wait for love."

"That is so sweet. See what I mean? This guy is so special and caring. How could I not marry this guy?" He leaned over and kissed me again.

"You two remind me of my husband and I when we first started out on this journey. I'm so excited for you both."

"I'm excited as well, Mrs. Moore." That was half of a lie. Truth is, I was taken aback by the whole situation, but I did have deep feelings for Anthony. I just didn't have the timetable that he had, obviously.

The night went smoothly after that. We talked about his childhood and my own, our careers. We continued to talk and eat and got to know each other. I was still nervous because this was not on my radar at all, but it all worked out.

"Well, Clayton, it was so nice to have met you." Anthony's father reached across the table to shake my hand again. "The wife and I have another engagement that we must get to, and we don't want to be late."

"Yes, we do. But this was so lovely and pleasant," his mother added.

We all pushed our chairs back and proceeded to gather our things.

"Come give your new mother a hug," Mrs. Moore requested. I walked around the table and embraced her in a tight hug. She had a nice firm grip on me. It was a loving one. I gently pulled back when I felt like enough time had elapsed.

"Welcome to the family, Clayton." She grabbed my hand and patted it. His father interjected with just a handshake.

I walked them all to their cars; then I pulled off in my own. I got home later that evening and lay across the bed with the events of today on my mind. Mainly the marriage part. I was surprised at the fact that over the time I was told I was getting married and up to now that how much more appealing it was becoming. I was in awe. I was thinking about marriage only after a few weeks.

My phone began to ring, and I picked it up.

"I'm sorry," were the first words that Anthony spoke to me.

"It's okay."

"No, it's not. That whole situation was a complete ambush." He sounded sorrowful.

"Wellllll . . . That is true, but I'm good with it now," I laughed. "I'm just glad that you didn't get down on one knee and propose to me. That could have been messy." I laughed a little.

"Again, I'm sorry."

"Anthony Moore, will you do me the honor of being my husband?" I spoke from my heart.

"Are you serious?" he sounded shocked.

"Absolutely. I meant what I said at the table earlier. As unconventional as this is, I do love you, sir. I am in love with you."

"Yes, I will marry you."

"Well, there you have it. We'll work out the details later. I have some work to do, so let today marinate, and I'll do the same. Love you."

"Love you too," he said, and then hung up the phone.

I looked at the phone on the bed for a few moments, hoping that I just did the right thing.

Chapter 35

Avery

Trust Issues

It is something to shake the hand of a known enemy, and it's another thing to not know. I had the upper hand and could take everything from him at any given moment. But it was all about timing and preparation. The way I would do it would be remembered for a long time to come.

I never thought about children, or the lack of, until now. I look at Corey and see possibilities. Don't get it twisted, I'm not going out to have sex with a female or pay someone to have my kid. Especially when there is one ripe for the picking underneath my nose. He was neglected by the father that loved him and hated him, but didn't know it. It was a card that I had. Another one to destroy a man and his home from the inside out. One that was among a few in my hand.

Running an empire and having multiple personas was pleasurable but exhausting, to say the least. Everything has a cost. Mine was sleep and comfort. I did not sleep much, and being comfortable means that I can be caught slipping. I didn't live in luxury, even though I had the wealth and power to do so. So, with all that being said, I wanted to reap some of those rewards without losing my life or freedom. I had one issue, though: trust. Who can you trust in this drug game? Almost no one. That is where Corey came in. Once I snatch him from his home and "rescue" him, he will owe me. He will owe me his trust. It will be a first time for me when it comes to my empire. I was close so many times to trusting someone, but something about them always disbanded my trust. I had a few tests for Corey that would let me know for sure if he could be trusted.

But first, I had to work his mother overtime. I had the package that she was waiting to get. She said she wanted the truth, but I was about to give her a lie. Even I was amazed at the work that the photo artist did with the photo shopped pictures. I looked at them a few times and then placed them in an envelope. I sealed them as to indicate that I never looked at them. That is what I was going to tell her. She needed someone that had her best interest at heart and someone that was impartial in the situation, because, quote/unquote, *I didn't know her husband.*

I pulled out my phone and called her number.

"Hey, Coach. How are you doing?" She had an upbeat voice, but I knew she was waiting for this call. She wanted to know if her husband had lived up to the standards that she set for him. I was happy to disappoint her.

"I'm taking it easy. One day at a time," I responded. "How are you doing today?" I asked, stalling on purpose.

"I'm doing quite wonderful for a woman on the edge."

"That's understandable." I was smiling on the other end of the phone. To have something that someone wanted, needed, and craved was feeding my ego right now.

"What are you doing right now?" I asked.

"I'm out shopping."

"Can we meet up in about an hour?"

"Yes, I have no problem with that." I could hear the anticipation in her words. She spoke hastily and with neediness in her voice.

"I'll text you the address in a minute. See you soon." I hung up the phone before she could get another word in.

Chapter 36

Leroy

Man-to-Man

I walked out of my house to my car with takeover heavy on my mind. I was growing more and more frustrated as the days went by. I got to my car and hopped in. Then I looked over to see a note on the inside of the windshield of the car. I reached out and pulled it off. I opened it and read the following:

I'm right under your nose. If you look hard enough, you just might find me. Man-to-man or maybe faggot-to-man.

Ghost

I was pissed that this muthafucker knew where I lived and somehow got access to my car. There was no need for me to have someone watching my house because I lived far away from where I did business. Now I was going to have to have surveillance at my house. I tried my best to keep my work away from my home, but now that this faggy bitch was upping the ante, I had to as well.

I banged the wheel in frustration. This moment took me back to a time when I received the most devastating news of my life.

I was about twelve or so, and I lived with my parents. I was an only child. We didn't live in the projects but close to them. Both of my parents worked jobs to keep a roof over our heads. I never wanted for anything except for name-brand things. My parents didn't feel the need to splurge on the higher priced and more popular shoes and clothes. Even though I didn't get the name-brand things, I had everything that I ever needed. I was an average student in a school located in the city. My father was a hardworking guy, and he made me proud to be his son. My parents had a good relationship from what I could see, but something changed, and one day, I came home and noticed that my father's things were gone. My father was a very great athlete, and in our living room, he had all his memorabilia and trophies in a corner with a chair beside it. They were gone as well, along with his plaques and certificates. I mean, *all* his things were gone, like he never existed. I searched the house in a panic just in case I was mistaken.

I was a latch-key child and almost always let myself in the house if my parents worked late or something like that. I was mature for my age and handled things differently for my age. I still messed up like all little boys my age, I just didn't go crazy.

Anyway, I got to my room and set my book bag on my bed and just sat on the bed. I usually would go get a snack from the refrigerator as soon as I got home, but that didn't happen today. I was dumbfounded and curious. Then I thought maybe we were moving, but then, why would only *his* stuff be gone I wondered. I wasn't sitting on my bed long before I heard the front door to the house open, and then the heavy footsteps of my father climbing the stairs. I got excited because I knew that he would have answers to questions that I had.

As soon as he walked into my room, I hopped off of the bed and ran over to him. I wrapped my arms around his waist like I hadn't seen him in weeks when just yesterday we sat down at the table for dinner. I didn't know that would be our last time.

"Hey, Roy," my father hugged me back. "How's my soldier?" I loved my father because we always had "man-to-man" conversations as he called them. I loved them and our bonding time.

I pulled back with a smile on my face and looked up to him in admiration. "Daddy, where are all of your things?"

"That's why I'm here. We need to talk. Sit down on the bed for me. We need to talk, man-to-man." I did as I was instructed. He, in turn, leaned up against one of my dressers with his hands in his pockets.

"Leroy, you know that Daddy loves you, right?"

"Yes, sir." I nodded my head. He told me he loved me very often.

"Well, Daddy has to move away for a little bit."

"Why?" I immediately got defensive and upset.

"It's hard to explain. Your mother and I have decided to live in separate places."

"Are y'all getting divorced?" I looked at him with fear in my eyes. A few tears welled up and then fell. My world was crumbling before me. He didn't answer right away. He looked away for a quick second.

"That is a possibility."

I sprang up off of the bed and ran over to him and gripped his waist again. I cried and begged him not to leave for over fifteen minutes. He promised that I would be able to come and stay with him as soon as he became stable. That day never came. I found out why because soon, my mother had to move from close to the projects into the projects. It was a huge shock and adjustment to us both. My mother cried and drank rather heavily after we moved in the projects. My attention declined toward my schoolwork, and I began to hang out with the rough guys that I steered clear of before we moved.

I was about fifteen when I found out that my father left my mother for a man. During one of her drinking fits, she came into my bedroom and spilled her guts on the whole situation. To say I was devastated was an understatement. I didn't want to believe it, so I called him one day and asked him. He told me the truth, and I hung up the phone on him. I haven't spoken to him since that day. I don't know if he's dead or alive. I didn't care. All I knew is that another man took my father from my mother and broke up a happy home. My fiery hatred for all gay men was fueled that day. I pulled off after going back down a very painful memory.

"How many of these faggots do I have to kill to get to this bastard?" I banged my hands on the table I was sitting at with some of my top men sitting in front of me. I was at one of my stash houses having another meeting. I was pissed that I was not getting anywhere with finding this dick taker. Maybe I was looking too hard.

"Any one of you have anything to tell me or show me? I need something to go on that will get me results." I looked around the table. No one opened their mouth. It infuriated me even more. I was paying these muthafuckers good money. They were eating well off my years of hard work, and here, they are silent.

"Since you old-ass fuckers in here can't help me, I'm getting some fresh blood in this to get this shit going. It's time to bring in the heir to the throne. It's time to bring my son on board. He's the key to this puzzle."

Chapter 37

Monica

Killing Me Softly

If I could have clicked my heels three times, I would have been where I wanted and needed to be in a second, but I wasn't a white bitch with a yappy dog chasing after her. I was a married kingpin's wife on the way to find out if her husband was missing two extra legs and a tail.

When Coach called me, I was in the middle of Saks Fifth Avenue in Arundel Mills Mall. I had a cart full of clothes and shoes that were calling me to buy them, but that didn't matter because as soon as he called me, I dropped everything and all my attention was on his voice on the other end of the phone. I tried my best not to sound desperate or needy, and I don't know if I succeeded in it, but I didn't care. He had something that I needed. I didn't even say a thing to the personal shopper that helped me pick out all the clothes for over a two-hour period. I would've been pissed off, but I didn't care about some young chick on commission right now. My sanity was on the brain at this point.

I was out of the store in seconds, and by the time I got to my car, I got the text that I was so desperately waiting to receive. It's amazing how only a few seconds can feel like a lifetime, especially when you are desperately waiting on something.

I pulled up to my destination with haste and exited my car. The place I pulled up to was a nice Italian restaurant with tons of people going in and out of it. I wasn't a big fan of Italian food, except for those that were Americanized. Anyway, I walked up to the maître d's podium to ask for my party but then realized that I didn't know the coach's name. I was embarrassed. I quietly and frantically looked past the gentleman and eyed the room in search of Coach. I quickly found him.

"Good day, madam. Welcome to Antonio's." The maître d' interrupted my frantic search.

"Good day as well," I greeted him and smiled. "My party is waiting on me over there." I pointed in the direction of Coach's table, but I didn't move. I was waiting to be escorted over to the table. My feet and mind threatened to say fuck the waiting, but I did have some manners and etiquette. I waited. He must have seen the angst on my face because he quickly moved and escorted me to the table with Coach.

"Monica." His smile was wide and jubilant. It put me at ease. He rose from his chair and pulled out a seat for me. I sat down with my mind going in circles. I saw wine at the table. It immediately started to call my name. Maybe it was the news that I was hoping not to find out. You know, that fact that your whole life with someone was a lie. That you possibly had to start over with someone else or live with the lie. My husband wouldn't be the first drug dealer with a chick on the side. I thought I was the exception. Maybe I wasn't.

I sat in silence for a few seconds, undecided on what to say.

"Monica, I'm sure you know why you are here now." Coach looked at me in the eyes. He was very good at concealing his feelings. I didn't know what to think.

"Yes, I do." I put on a big-girl smile, but on the inside, I was a wreck. At this moment, I couldn't even go with that "gut feeling" they say all women have. That shit was a lie that some uneducated muthafucker fed to us, but that's not relevant right now.

"Well, I brought you here, out in public, so that you could have someone here just in case it is not the news that you want. I told my guy to seal the envelope so that you were the only one to see the photos. I did it out of sensitivity of the situation and your privacy."

"I respect and appreciate that gesture." I still had the weak smile on my face. I had been through murders, kidnapping, drug deals gone bad, and child birth, but this shit was killing me softly as Lauryn Hill so eloquently sang the song.

He placed the envelope on the table, tapped his hand on it, and slid it across the table to me. I felt the envelope as it entered my space. My fingers latched on to it like I was an angry octopus. I slid it toward me. The paper felt soft underneath my fingers. I looked down at it and willed it to open itself. I couldn't do it. After all this time, waiting and filling up the empty time with nonsense just to get to this point, and then freeze up!

"Are you okay?" Coach asked. His eyes were filled with understanding.

"Yes, I'm . . ." I took a deep breath and then spoke, "No, I'm not good. I thought that I was in a better place than this. I trust my husband. I trusted my husband. I've been losing my mind over these last few days, and it has now come down to this. I'm the desperate chick with trust issues. I said that I never would be her or one of them. Now look at me. I had my husband followed, tracked, and traced. This is not normal."

"Normal is overrated. Plus, it's you protecting yourself. No one can tell you what to do after you find out whatever you find out, but don't beat yourself up for getting proof. You will sleep better at night knowing the truth, whether or not it be what you want."

I heard what he said, and I agreed, but it didn't make this situation any easier.

I picked up the envelope and carefully pulled it open. I was still stalling for time. I was mostly trying to control the reaction on my face. Fear was winning right at this moment. I finally had it opened; then I pulled out one of the pictures. I didn't say anything as I looked at the picture. I pulled out another one and another one. There were about twelve pictures in total. I stacked them in a nice neat pile and put them back in the envelope. I was numb. I wasn't in denial or disbelief. Just numb.

"Monica?" Coach called out my name in a calm and concerned voice. It was like he could see through my mask.

"She can have him." Those were the first words that came out of my mouth. The woman's face was blurred out. But it had them kissing, and it wasn't innocent. There were no bedroom pictures, so I don't know if they had sex or not, but I will never know who she is because of the hidden identity. I guess it was for her safety and not my sanity. Because every woman that I see from now on will be a suspect. It will be a never-ending whirlwind of suspects and bed hoppers.

"You're not thinking clearly. That is pain talking."

"Have you ever had someone you loved and dedicated your life to cheat on you?" I looked at him in anger. He didn't say a thing, but I continued in a low but serious tone. "Fuck no, so don't tell me what is talking until you have been there."

"First, he didn't cheat on you. He cheated himself. You're taking the victim seat when you are not. And second, you don't know about me because I didn't choose to share it. But I know pain. We are very close." He was firm and comforting at the same time. I felt bad.

"I'm sorry. You're right." I felt like shit twice over. He did me a favor—then I attacked him like it was his fault.

"Don't apologize. I totally understand."

"Can you keep this between us? Corey is in a good place, and I don't want him to do something stupid to his father. I want to process this and handle this on my own."

"That's something that you don't have to worry about."

He offered to buy me dinner, but I wasn't in the mood. I just wanted to go home. He walked me to my car but handed me two bottles of wine "to get me through the night." I prayed that it would help with the pain that I was feeling. I would be seeing the bottom of the bottle from the top tonight for sure.

Chapter 38

Corey

Two Birds

We had just won another game, and I was amped up. My father wasn't at the game like the last one, but he sent Dre as a replacement and my mother, who was rather distant. She's been like that for a few weeks. I think it started when my father blacked out on her on the patio a couple of weeks ago. I know it changed her. Dre and I dropped my mother off and did what came natural to us, even though we had to be superdiscreet with what was going from an understanding to a relationship. Dre was older than me by some years. Yet, we still could relate. He was cool to be around, and he was laid-back too. He didn't require much.

"So, you are the son of a drug dealer. You want to be the heir to the throne?" Dre asked.

I wondered where that question came from. It was out of the blue. We had just finished having sex and lay next to each other in silence. Once again, we had picked a motel that was miles away from where we lived or did business. We made sure we would mix up the locations that we went to and how long we stayed. Maybe it was the guilt of the situation. Him fucking his boss's son was not on the list of things to do, yet, he still took the chance. It made me confident that he had some feelings vested.

"I never really thought about it." We didn't look at each other when we talked. It was just words between two guys. "I was born into this. It wasn't my choice."

"So what you gonna do, the basketball thing?"

"I can say that I never really thought that far ahead."

"You need to be thinking about your future. You need to choose. Your father is getting ready to ask you. You need to have an answer and soon." His voice was even-toned and serious.

"I will."

"This is your life. Your decisions are not just for you. They are for others. Choose carefully. Neither choice is for the faint of heart, and both can take a toll on you. One is more physical, and the other is more mental."

"What would you do?" I asked.

"I can't give you any answers. Your life and my life are two different ones. Two different paths that happened to connect at one point and will travel until the time is up for our conjoined paths. Do what is pleasing to you and no one else. You only get to make this decision once."

"Okay," I answered. There was some silence in the room for a few minutes as we just lay there. I was hoping that he would give me some help, but he didn't. He was not going to help me, and I wasn't the begging type. We both, almost at the same time, began to get dressed. Again, few words were spoken as we left the hotel and made our way back to our destinations.

I walked in the house to some music playing and my mother sitting in the living room with a glass of wine in her hand. She had been doing this for the past few days, but I didn't choose to address it until today.

"Ma, are you okay?" I asked as I walked around the side of the couch and in front of where she was sitting. She had the wineglass in hand, and she swirled it.

"Why do you ask that, Corey?" She looked like she was in another world as she talked.

"Because all you do is drink wine and sit on this couch every time I come home." I sat down next to her with most of my body positioned toward her.

"I like wine. It keeps me stable. I love it, and it loves me."

I took the wine away from her and placed it on the coffee table close to us. "You don't need any more of this.

"Are you going to tell me what's wrong with you?" I asked.

She turned her head toward me but said nothing. I could see tears forming in the corner of her eyes, but they wouldn't fall. They only threatened to. My mother is a tough lady, and to see her here on the verge of tears was very disturbing to me. It had something to do with my father. I felt it, but she wasn't going to say anything because she was loyal to this man, my father, no matter what. She was a ride-or-die chick. I didn't know the hold that my father had on her, but it was a tight one. One could say it was unbreakable.

"Corey, are you dating someone?" The question caught me off guard. This was supposed to be about her right now, but suddenly, the wind has shifted in my direction. I wasn't ready for this.

"Ummmm . . ." I didn't know how to respond.

"I know that you are. Basketball is only consuming part of your time. I know that you are having one of your father's men to drive you to hook up with them. I understand. I've been there and done that. Just don't give your heart and body to the wrong one. Make sure they are in it for the long haul. Don't break their hearts either. Be a man about it and let them know if you are not happy."

I just nodded my head in agreement. I can say that I was truly confused now.

"Did my father do something to you again? Because if he did, I will fucking kill him." Anger rose in me with a fiery passion.

"Your father isn't responsible for this hurt. I am. I'm to blame for my pain right now. I'll be all right, Corey. I know I will."

"You sure?" I didn't believe her, and I was going to be doing some investigation soon enough. I've got to get to the bottom of this.

"I have no doubt in my mind. Everything will all right." She reached over to the coffee table and picked up her glass of wine and continued to sip as she did when I first arrived.

Now I had an even bigger decision to make. Either pursue this negativity that I know my father is bringing my mother's way or accept his offer to join him in the ranks. Shit, I'll do both. Kill two birds with one stone.

Chapter 39

Clayton

Shotgun

I had everything set. I was going against everything that I would normally do. Being that I just got engaged a few weeks ago, this was something that I was surprised to be doing. I made a few calls over the last two weeks and got everything in order. I can say that I was very excited. I just hoped that everything would go as planned.

His parents helped me get his friends and family to where we were headed.

"I'm so glad that you could come with me. I'm sure this will be a night that you won't forget." I looked over at Anthony as I continued to drive toward our destination. I told him that we were going to some type of Policeman's Ball so he could get dressed in his best for the day. Night weddings aren't ideal, but I had to make it work. We hadn't even worked out the details about living arrangements, but that wouldn't be too hard. I didn't own where I lived, so more than likely, I would share his home with him. It would be a bump up for me. He did have good taste in furniture and all of that. I was no slouch, but I knew when to concede in areas that I was indeed no competition.

Anyway, I had the best wedding planner in Maryland do the wedding based off the color schemes of Anthony's living room, and it was out of this world. He sent me pictures that blew my mind away. I was so excited and nervous at the same time. All this cost plenty of money, and a ton of favors was called in for the last-minute arrangements, but it all worked out.

"I hope you can dance because I don't want you stepping on my feet," Anthony said, and then laughed.

"I'm gay, so you know I'm naturally light on my feet," I joked. He laughed. His laugh made me feel at ease. It made me feel like I was doing the right thing tonight.

We finally pulled up to the address of the venue where the wedding was being held. It was not decorated on the outside for various reasons. Mainly, I didn't want to give anything away.

"You ready to go? This is the first time that I have a man to go to these things with." I looked him in the eyes as I spoke. I was sincere as I spoke. He looked at me with an unwavering gaze. It made my heart melt. I was in love for sure. No one could tell me differently. I was missing my parents at this moment, but now, there was someone to fill the void. I would shower with love and spoil him for years to come. I was sure of it.

I finally got out of the car and rushed around to the other side of the vehicle to help him out. I wanted him to feel special for eternity.

We walked side by side up to the door; then I opened the door and let him enter first. There was a person there with a tuxedo on to greet us as if this was the real thing.

"You ready?" I looked at him in the eyes once again.

"I was made to flaunt. Let's get this, baby." He kissed me on the cheek. And then the doors were opened for us on cue.

Applauds and whistles rang out as we walked in. The room was filled with red and white roses all over, and all 150 guests were dressed in red and white. Anthony was in a state of shock. He didn't move but a few feet after we came through the door. There was a banner hanging over the center of the aisle that said. *"Congratulations, Mr. and Mr. Moore."*

"You did this?" he asked as tears freely ran down both his cheeks.

"All for you, baby. I couldn't wait another minute to be with you."

He moved in closer and kissed me on the lips. It was a long and passionate one. The applauds and whistling started up once again.

I softly pulled away from him. "Baby, we have to go and get married now."

"Okay," he said as he sniffed back some tears; then we walked down the aisle to the official that oversaw the service.

We officially became one, and both Anthony and I cried ourselves crazy during the rest of the night. I guess it was the best day for both of us.

Chapter 40

Avery

Associates

"Monica, what are you doing right now?"

"What am I doing?" she repeated my question back to me. It was a pet peeve of mine, and I knew that she comprehended quite well, but I ignored it and moved on. She was a part of my plan, and nothing she did could remove her from my grip.

"I need you to get dressed and meet me at the address I will send you in a few minutes. This is a formal event, so dress to kill." I didn't let her respond before I hung up the phone. I knew that she would be there. She wasn't doing anything anyway. Her husband was her life, and even with the information she had, she still wouldn't leave him. She was what the streets called ride or die. She was in it for the long haul. It was an admirable quality for one to have. It was also a curse. You commonly lose your own life with loyalty to another, especially with a street hustler for a husband. It's in the small print of the invisible contract.

I was invited out to a wedding party by a friend. He was married a few days ago. It was a surprise wedding for his lover. The wedding banquet was being held days after it. It was unconventional but innovative at the same time. That's why he was on my team.

Monica pulled up to the destination, stepped out of the car, all decked out in a dress that seduced even my dick to stand up at attention. It was a *come-hither* dress. It was a fishing-for-attention dress. Meaning, she was fishing for some compliments and accolades. She was trying to fill a void. She was a knockout-gorgeous chick. Her husband was crazy to be ignoring her for these streets and the fame he was chasing. I watched as she checked herself in the car mirror quickly. I tapped my car horn, alerting her of my presence. I then exited my car and made my way to where she was standing.

"You look very nice," I said as I greeted her. She smiled. I know that she needed to hear that.

"Thank you very much. You don't look scruffy yourself." She rubbed her hand across my chest. She didn't know that she was trying to shake the wrong tree. She looked a bit drunk or high. Maybe it was the wine that I was giving her from time to time. She didn't know it, but it was laced with the cough syrup that some of the kids were getting high with right now. And it was highly addictive. All it took was a syringe filled with the promethazine shot into the cork at the top of the bottle. With the cork already having holes in it, no one was the wiser. I said that I was going to ruin Leroy's house from the inside out, and I meant it. I liked her, but she was a casualty of war or the game. It wasn't a war because both sides should have a chance at winning. Leroy didn't. He was too headstrong and self-centered. He was at a disadvantage because he didn't know what I looked like because he had what I should look like already established in his mind. That is also the reason why he didn't know that his son was gay. He had too much of the wrong evidence.

Anyway, I took Monica's hand into my own, and we walked into my friend Anthony's home, where the event was taking place.

Monica's facial expression was one of awe as she stepped into the house of my friend and now his husband's house. There was light jazz playing and many guests walking around with drinks in their hands. I didn't know anyone there but Anthony and Monica, and that was the way it was going to stay. I was charming and secretive at the same time. It got me by all these years and has not yet failed me.

"This place is beautiful. I mean, you can tell that this place has a woman's touch." I didn't want to burst her bubble with her misinformation because she would soon find out on her own.

There were quite a few gay men at this event, and she would soon see for herself.

We made our way through a few rooms. There was one room with some art and statues in it and some people admiring the style. I personally didn't care for it. Monica, on the other hand, paused and started to admire it as well. Then we passed by a room that looked like a small library with old-fashioned ladders that latched onto the bookshelves and could be used to explore the collection of books, no matter the height. After the small tour, we made it to the room where Anthony was sitting in a chair with a few people surrounding him. His husband Clayton was there as well with a bright smile on his face.

"Clarence, so glad you could make it." He stood up and gave me a tight hug around the neck. It was just a show. He was more of a business partner than a friend. He had a contract and a mutual understanding. The money I paid him for his work paid for all of this. "I'm pretty sure you remember Clayton," he said as he turned toward Clayton, and then gently kissed him on the cheek with affection. This was an act on both Anthony and our parts. This was just formality.

"Yes, and it is so nice to see him one more time." I reached out toward him and shook his hand. Clayton was the detective that was looking for me and Monica's husband. He was clueless, to say the least, or he didn't play his hand. I didn't hate him or any of that. I hated when others were getting in my way. Knowingly and unknowingly. It was all going per plan anyway. Everybody had a part and was playing it well. Most didn't even know they were being used. Namely, Monica and Clayton.

"And who is this bombshell beauty beside you?" Anthony asked in curiosity. I thought about saying, *the weak competition's wife*, but said, "Monica is a close friend of mine."

"Hello, Anthony, it's so nice to meet you. And your house is quite beautiful," she said as she stuck out her hand to greet him.

"It's nice to meet you as well, and thank you so much for the compliment. It took me forever to get this house to look the way I wanted it."

"I need the number of your decorator because she did a fabulous job with this place," Monica gushed.

"He's standing right in front of you," Anthony smiled, and then laughed. So did a few others that were around us.

"Oh Lord, I didn't mean to be offensive." She looked at me with slight embarrassment on her face.

"Don't worry, honey. It was an honest mistake. I'm over it. I'm so glad to meet you, and I hope that you enjoy yourself in my humble abode."

"I will, and thank you so much for having me."

"I'll talk to you later. We're going to mingle a bit." I winked at Anthony and gently ushered Monica away from that group of people. I wasn't embarrassed by her or her statement, but I didn't want her to dig a deeper ditch with her mouth. She had quite a bit in common with her husband for sure. Those assumptions will certainly get you in trouble.

"Thank you so much for rescuing me from that. I really put my foot in my mouth that time." She patted me on the leg as we were seated on one of Anthony's sofas.

"Monica, you were being human, and that's all there is to that," I said, hoping it would make her feel better. It was the truth.

"I'm so glad that you invited me to this party. It got my mind off my troubles." She had a sincere look on her face. It was mixed with a glimpse of pity as well.

"It was my pleasure. Believe me."

"My husband would be blowing a gasket right now if he knew that I was at a party celebrating the marriage of two men."

"Is he homophobic?"

"He's beyond homophobic. I can't even describe his disdain for men who sleep with other men." She looked at me with gloom.

"Well, let's not tell him about it then. We'll keep it our little secret."

"Most definitely," she said, and then let out a hearty laugh.

"Now, where can a sister get a drink of wine around here?"

There was a server going around with a tray in her hand. I signaled to her, and she came toward us. We both grabbed a glass, and Monica immediately began to drink hers. I could tell that she was now addicted to it.

"It's not as good as the ones that you give me, but it'll do."

"Yeah, I get mine from a special supplier. I have a few bottles in the trunk of my car for you to take home."

"Really? I can't wait to crack one of those open when I get home. Or maybe before."

"I hear that." I smiled on the outside but laughed on the inside. She was an addict and didn't even know it.

Chapter 41

Leroy

Joining the Ranks

I was so glad that my son was now sitting at the table with me and my crew. It felt good to have him here, knowing that he was the heir to the throne. I didn't want to have to force him to do it. Truth is, he came to me before I could even ask him. It was one of those days that I was home trying to relax. I had hit Monica off in the bedroom again the night before and was relaxing on the back porch once again. I was still plotting and planning but not as heavy as I would if I was around my men.

"Dad, we need to talk." He came over to where I was sitting and pulled out a chair. My son was becoming a man, and I could see it in the way he walked and the way he talked. He had my stride, and the deepness of his voice almost matched my own. He was a spitting image of me and his mother when it came to physical appearance. He had her smile and small ears. I just didn't know where he was mentally. Corey was a very independent child and now teen. As an only child, we worried, mainly me, about him being a productive child. I'm so glad that he is. He is outgoing, into sports and most things a male child would do, like girls and video games. I loved seeing him play in sports and the like, but I knew that he didn't need me there to perform well. He made me proud.

"Sure, son, what's up?" I turned all my attention to him.

"I want in." He had a serious look on his face. It was unflinching.

"What do you mean?" I asked. I knew what he meant. I just wanted to hear him say it.

"I want in on the drug game. It's about time I get in and get rooted. I want to help you with this takeover. We can take the streets if we double-team it. I'm sure of it."

I wanted to jump out of the chair and grab him into a big hug, but I kept my cool and looked at him in silence for a few moments.

"Son, that's the best news that I've heard in a long time. I'm so glad that you came to this decision. You are, without a doubt, my seed. I knew that you would follow in my steps, and I'm proud to have you aboard."

"Dad, it was the only right thing to do, and the time is now. I'm about to finish school soon; then, it was either basketball or the drug game. The game was the only choice since my father already was poised to take the top. Why not sit next to the king?"

"That's cool, son. You don't know what your father goes through to keep his family in the lifestyle they're accustomed to having. It's not a cake walk. You understand?"

"I am all in for this shit, Dad. I come from good stock, and I'm made tough for the streets. I'm in it to win it. They ain't going to see us coming. We got this, Dad. Just train me and set me loose."

"Cool, I'm going to put you with my boy Dre so he can begin to show you the ropes. It won't take you long to catch on; then soon, we can start bringing you into the round table and putting some fresh ideas on table. That's what we need. You're the next generation, and we'll take all."

I reached out my hand and shook his, and that's all I needed to lift my spirits.

Chapter 42

Monica

Liar, Liar

My husband had been in a good mood lately. Mainly because my son told him that he would join his empire. I was all for a father-son relationship, but I didn't feel too happy about my son lining up with a liar. I've been having sex with my husband as a duty only and not to lead to any type of suspicions. I had evidence that I almost always looked at daily. It was not a good thing to do, but I did it anyway. I was almost obsessed. Every chick that I saw on the street that resembled the body of that chick I wanted to punch in the face. But since the face of the chick was blurred a bit, I couldn't get a positive identification . . . or that chick would be dead by now. I should shoot myself. Because I was so stupid enough to believe my own hype, I was more depressed that I lied to myself all of these years than anything that Roy had done. Don't get it twisted. I still wanted payback. I just wanted it my way. I wanted him to remember the person that stood by him all these years, and he shit on my face. I wanted him to remember forever. I could have my brothers, who work for him, dismember his ass, but that would be too easy on him. I wanted him be alive to suffer for a long time.

I have come to grips with the fact that I'm a liar to myself. And that he was a liar in general.

I wanted to know what I did to merit such treatment. I mean, I was faithful. I trained our son, and I did advance on any of the flirtatious men that came my way. I was a bomb-ass chick, and many men knew it too. But, no, I always turned them down and kept my vows to my husband—and this is where it got me.

I am a booze hound, or a lush, as they call it. Addicted to wine. I had it morning, noon, and night. I have always been a wine drinker, but I don't ever remember it giving me such a high that it does now. I assume it's the brand that Coach/Clarence has been giving me. It helps me cope with my day.

I can't believe how much Coach has been there for me. I mean, he is such a great guy. He answers the phone almost every time I call, training my son in his father's frequent absences, and the wine, of course. I wonder if he's married. I was thinking he may be gay after the party that we went to the other day. But that would be making him guilty by association, and I don't want to put my foot in my mouth once again. I decided to call him and ask him. That was always the best thing to do.

I picked up my cell phone and pressed his contact to call him.

"Hello," he answered after a few rings.

"Clarence, I was just calling to tell you thank you for taking me out the other day. I had such a fantastic time."

"Monica, that was a pleasure for me to do. It was my intention to get your mind off your troubles."

"Clarence, that isn't the only reason I'm calling you." I was a little nervous about asking this question. It was a personal question, and it could lead to all types of speculations and other things.

"Okay, what's the reason you're calling me?"

"Well." I paused and took a sip of wine from the glass that was in front of me. That liquid courage statement was very true. "Are you married or involved with anyone."

"Yes, I am married," he answered.

I breathed a sigh of relief.

"I was asking because you never talk of anyone, and I was just wondering why a good guy like you would take me out to a party with you."

"Truthfully, Monica, my wife doesn't enjoy those types of things, and she is very comfortable with me having female friends. She encourages it, actually."

"Wow. How long have you two been married?"

"Well, it seems like forever." He laughed, and I did as well. "But, we have been going strong for twenty years."

"That's very inspiring to hear."

"It wasn't easy, and it's still work. But I love her and wouldn't trade her for the world."

"Do you have any advice for my husband and me? Seeing as you know some of the details?"

"Monica, I did a favor for you as a favor, but I don't give advice on relationships. You have to make decisions for yourself."

"I understand. I'm sorry I asked." Now I felt crazy for asking.

"Don't be. It was just a question."

"Well, I don't want to hold you. Besides, my husband just walked in the door. I'll talk to you later." I hung up the phone to hide my shame.

Coincidentally, my husband did walk in the door, even though I just lied to get off the phone with Coach.

"Hey, baby, how was your day?" I said. I got up off the sofa and walked toward him. I kissed him on the lips with a long passionate kiss. Just to remind him of who I was and what I should mean to him.

"It was business as usual. Hustle and flow. You know how I do." My husband was a good-looking man. I can see why the chick in the picture went after him.

"That's good. Let me greet my man in style." I dropped to my knees and immediately went for his pants. He had on sweatpants, so it was easy for me to pull them down, pull out his dick, and go to work. This was something that I used to do when we first started out, and I thought he needed another reminder.

I worked him over so good that he came in my mouth within minutes.

"Damn, Monica," he said laboring to breathe. "That was one hell of a greeting. I don't know what I would do without you on my side. What man could ask for a better wife?" He smiled as he pulled his clothes back up.

"Nobody but you, baby." I kissed him on the lips again. I wanted to say, *an honest man,* but I kept my comment and composure to myself. I followed up with a fresh bath for him and a home-cooked meal. He would never be able to say I didn't play my position, even if I was pretending to be what I wanted him to be: faithful. This ride-or-die shit was for the birds. I don't know how long I was going to be able to hold on and not explode. We shall see.

Chapter 43

Corey

Confidant

"Coach, you have a minute?" I sprinted up to Coach who was on the other side of the gym. We had just finished a practice session a day or two before one of our games. The team had just put the equipment away and was ready to go home. Even though I told my father that I would be a part of the family business, I still wanted to talk to someone impartial about my choice. Coach was an approachable person, even though he had a hard-on for being on point and about his business. I just needed someone to talk to. I talked to Dre, but he was too close to the game, and he was not very helpful.

"What can I do for you, son?" he looked at me with an expressionless face as usual. I don't think he didn't care. I just thought he was a master at keeping it neutral. I wanted to learn how to do that. It was an asset to have.

"Can we talk in private?"

"Sure, let's go in my office."

I followed behind him and couldn't help but notice his firm ass through his pants. I refocused myself as I got to the office and sat in the chair. I don't know what it is about an older man that catches my eye.

"So what can I help you with?" he asked.

"I've made a decision, and I need another point of view."

"Okay, let's have at it."

"Well, you know I love sports and basketball too, but there was another offer on the table. It was a decision based on some things that I will discuss later. My father wanted me to become a part of the family business. It's not your typical business, though."

"What do you mean by that?"

"Well . . ." I paused because while the family business provided well for me, I was not very open about it. How do you tell someone that your family helps people escape misery for another misery? A misery that destroys lives in the process? "I don't know quite how to say it."

"Just say it."

"Coach, if I tell you this, your life is in danger if you let it get out. That's not a threat. It's just what it is." I looked at him as I wore the same emotionless face that he wore on a regular basis.

"Corey, danger is in everyday life. I'm not worried about danger."

Everything in me was telling me not to do this. Not to mention this. To change the subject. To act as if I was retarded or act like I suddenly got sick so I should leave. Maybe I can act like my phone rang and I must take it outside, and then just dip off. But then I couldn't come back because he would still want to know what I wanted to tell him whenever I returned. I liked this team and this time is my life. This one moment could change everything for me. I wanted to fucking kill myself. My father would probably disown me—or kill me for even mentioning our way of life or how we have everything that we do.

"Okay, my pop's is a drug kingpin, and he wants me to sit at the table with him. I'm cool with the drug part, for the most part, but I don't trust my pops as far as I can throw him."

"Is there a reason for this lack of trust?" he asked, without batting an eye. I wanted to ask "Did you fucking *hear* what I just said to you?" But I didn't.

"Well, my pops has been on this takeover of the city tirade and trying to find and take out this gay kingpin guy so he can have the whole city."

"That's it?" He still looked unfazed by all that I was saying. Like it wasn't a big deal.

"No, he has been on the streets more than ever, and when he's home, he's on some lunatic shit. About two times my mother has told me, he has been physical with her. I don't mean abusive or beating her ass. But he has put his hands on her, and I am not cool with that. I'm pissed at him. I want to cut his balls off and stuffed them in his mouth. What would you do if it were you?"

"That's not something that I can answer for you."

"What the hell does that mean?" I had an attitude that I was shooting at the wrong person.

"That means you going to have to do a man-to-man thing with your father. You want to be at the table. Earn the damn position. If you mad about it, then be about it. Shit or get off the pot."

I looked at him for a moment and then nodded my head in agreement. He said he couldn't answer it for me, but he did. I liked this dude.

"Coach, thanks for listening. I'll be playing on the team until the end, just to let you know."

"I see you know about danger too." He laughed. I laughed as well. It was safe to say that Coach was a true friend and a person I could trust. I hoped.

Chapter 44

Clayton

Day One

I awoke in a strange yet comfortable bed this morning. It was the bed that I now shared with my husband. I was so glad to be able to put my house up for sale and put my things in storage that I almost skipped around that day. I only brought along a few of my things besides my clothes. Anthony had what they call a small McMansion that had many rooms in it. I have only been in a few rooms, but they were all fabulous and exquisitely decorated. I almost didn't want to touch anything. I was here alone. He was on call and got called to the hospital today.

Again, I was amazed at the setup of Anthony's home. It was very well done. The people in his life were seemingly on the same wave length with him. The wedding party the other day was eye opening. He had some very conceited friends. They didn't look down on me per se, but you could tell that they were hard to please and had "different" taste. I wasn't a fish out of water. I was just a bit thrown by some of their standoffish ways. It wasn't direct, but you could tell. It could have been me feeling out of place, though, but I am planning on getting used to this life, plus, once I bust this case wide open, I'll be capable of bringing more to the table.

Anyway, I sat up on the mattress and then eased down off the high canopy bed. I slid into some slippers that were on the floor beside the bed. They were so soft and felt like I was walking on air. Today was the last day of leave for my "honeymoon," and I was going to enjoy it too. I wasn't off work even though I was not in my office. I checked my e-mails from my phone like most people, but I also read some newspapers that covered stories from the city like murders, fires, disappearances, kidnappings, and various other crimes. There were always clues in them that helped me get closer to my goal.

My stomach churned, letting me know that I needed to go to the bathroom. I walked down the hall to where the bathroom was. I haven't been through his house thoroughly, but the bathroom was one place I remembered.

I walked in the very large bathroom and sat down on the bowl that was pristine and lovely. I didn't know a toilet could look so good. Then I exited the bathroom feeling very light. I was hungry, so I made my way down the stairs and toward the kitchen.

Anthony said that he had someone come to cook and clean for him from time to time. I guess today wasn't one of those days. Once again, I admired Anthony's taste in décor. The kitchen had stainless steel appliances and marble everything. And it all sparkled like one of those virtual house tours you saw online. I was so giddy inside. I had a man and one with money and good looks too. I didn't mind not being the one with the money for the time being. I am going to enjoy this life.

I pulled out some turkey bacon, eggs, and some shredded potatoes I saw and made me a meal fit for a king. I cleaned as I cooked so that I wouldn't come across as the slob that I could be. I sat down at the six-seat glass kitchen table and dined on my breakfast in my new home. One would even think that it tasted better in this setting, but maybe that was just me being overly exaggerating.

I finished my meal and then decided to give myself a tour of the house. I was an investigator by nature, so I was easily intrigued by the newness.

I went back up the stairs and decided to look in the rooms that I hadn't had a chance to peek into. There were several rooms. The first two I opened the door to were just bedrooms; then there was a closet type room that was for his clothes. I looked at all the impressive and expensive-looking clothes on racks and hangers. There were shoe walls from head to toe along one side of the wall and a huge mirror that let you see you from almost all angles.

I made my way out of that room after trying on a few things and then did my best to put them back the way I found them. I then walked down to the end of the hall and the room a few doors down from the bedroom. It was his home office. It was a standard-sized office that had a fabulous touch of class to it. I went and sat down in his chair behind his desk and marveled at the posh quality of Anthony's life once again.

"Shit, I'm in the wrong profession," I said, and then laughed at my own humor. It made me wonder how much he made for a living. I didn't get to wonder much longer because something caught my eye hanging on the wall. It was a picture that I recognized very well. It was *Biàn tài,* or the symbol for it, that is. I stood up and then saw it again as I looked down at the rug that was on the floor. My mouth hung open in awe. And curiosity drove me to travel around the house and in each room. There was a small sample of it on something, a wall clock, pillow, or a vase.

I ended up sitting in the living room with my mind almost spinning at full speed.

"This can't be. This *isn't* what it looks like," I said to myself. "Maybe this was a coincidence. Maybe he was just in love with Asian symbols or something like that." I rubbed my now throbbing temples because I was utterly confused.

"Who am I sleeping with?" I said, and then put my head in my hands.

Chapter 45

Avery

Fire

I spent most of my day on my compound and in my office. I was liking the way that my empire was growing. I was bringing in the numbers, and the money was giving me life. I had some casualties on the streets because Leroy was still trying his best to find me or get someone to talk. I laughed at how tenacious this man was and at his hard-on for me. He didn't know that he was chasing an image that he built in his head. He would never find me that way. Again, straight was straight, but gay had many faces. I'm so glad that I had his son in my grasp. I was letting Corey think that he would be working for his father, but that was to get him to get all the information that I needed to swallow up Leroy and his whole business—and his son and wife with him.

I loved a well-executed plan and one that would give me all power. I went back over my day with Monica a few days ago at the party and marveled at her gullibility and vulnerability when it came to her and her family. All of them were clueless, though. She was becoming a full-fledged junkie under my care and guidance, and I was using her loneliness as a weapon against her without her knowledge. Every time she came to a game with her son, she left with a special "treat" from me in the form of a bottle of wine. My chemist was a master at making drugs inconspicuous and in all types of forms. That cough syrup was highly addictive but almost undetectable in taste mixed with something else.

There were so many forms of different types of drugs floating around and being sold from my camp that would make it impossible for the police to get a grip on it. I was in heaven at the mayhem that I was at the wheel of. And the power to control a city and drug empire with such ease gave me a raw and unadulterated high that no physical drug could ever come close to. Power was my raw drug of choice. I'm about to turn up the fire.

Chapter 46

Leroy

Drunk in Love

I was excited to finally have my boy on my team. I didn't want to force him to do something that he didn't want to do, but it was something I wanted him to do. There is nothing like your son taking a spot next to you in the family business. Even though this isn't your "normal" father and son business, it was a business nonetheless.

Things were falling into place rather nicely, and I was driven even more now that my son was going to be adding to the equation. I was driving through the city with my boy, Dre, in the passenger seat of the car.

"Yo, son, this shit is about to get real in this city. Them fags are going down now. I got some young blood at the table. Corey is just like his pops; a hustler at heart. I can tell by the way he carries the ball on the court and the way his team and coach admire him. They know a born leader when they see one," I boasted.

"True dat." Dre nodded his head in agreement. Dre was a man of little words. When he spoke, I listened. I didn't want a motormouth on my team. If you got too much to say on my team, then you were at risk to run it to the wrong people. "Loose lips sink ships" was applicable in most situations, and in this one, it could cost you your life.

"Dre, when are you going to spread a seed into the earth so you can pass on your legacy?"

"Bro, that's not even been on my radar right now. I want the right one to bear my seed. They haven't come around yet, so I ain't moving or hopping on anything at the moment. Time got the cards. I just play what I'm dealt."

"Dude, you are right about that. I'm glad I got the lady that I have. I couldn't have a better wife in my life. She's got my back no matter what, and I need it in this business. Now, my son in the mix and all is well, dude. I feel a change coming, and I believe it's in my favor, bro."

"You got that, bro. Change *is* coming." He nodded his head once again. I'm glad for brothers like him. I didn't have any biological ones that I know of. He was one of the closest things to it.

"This you, dude," I said as I pulled up next to his car and watched him get out and hop in his joint. We almost never parked in the same place twice. That was key to staying alive in the game. I keep my circle small.

It took me about twenty minutes to get to my house doing high speeds getting home. I had an urge to be with my wife in a special way. And the way that she has been treating me the other day, I will welcome the services that she does so well.

I pulled up to the house, and I noticed that her car was gone. I hoped that it was Corey who had it and not her because my libido was on blast right now.

I exited my car rather quickly, but I looked around to make sure I wasn't being followed or anything. You can't be too sure. I had someone watching my house for a bit, and then let it go for a few days. I wanted to appear off guard, but I had something in the wings. I had something better than people watching. Technology was on point, and I used it to guard my house better than any person could.

Anyway, I entered my home with a pep in my step. I was glad to be home. My dick was already semihard at the thought of the looming ecstasy. My wife had the best pussy in the world.

I heard some jazz playing as soon as I entered the house. It meant she was in a good mood.

"Baby!" I hollered out. I almost started to undress on my way to her, but I didn't want to seem overly eager to get it. I wanted her to work for it. I knew that she would want it that way. She was a please-your-man type of lady, and I was a fitting king if I do say so myself.

After I didn't get an answer, I decided to look for her myself. My voice was a commanding voice, but the music was playing somewhat loudly.

I found her in the living room and what I saw was something I didn't like at all.

"Monica," I yelled, but she didn't hear me. She was slumped over on the chair like an addict with a wineglass and bottle in front of her.

"Monica!" I yelled again as I walked over to where the music was playing and cut it off. I yelled her name again. Still no response.

I got up close to her and kneeled in front of her. She was slumped over like a man trying to suck his own dick. I was immediately pissed. I knew what this look was, and I thought the worst.

I lightly began to tap her face to awaken her, and when that didn't happen, I did a full-fledged slap to the face.

She popped up in shock.

"Why you hit me like that?" she asked as she slowly rubbed her face. She looked angrier than I was now.

"Because your ass was bent the fuck over like a crackhead," I scolded her. "What the fuck is wrong with you?"

"What the fuck is wrong with *you?*" she came back at me with the same attitude I was giving her. We almost never talked like this to each other. I only did it when I was pissed with her or at something on the street. Most of the time it was out of frustration.

"Monica, you doing too much drinking. If I didn't know any better, I would have thought that you were high."

"High?" She looked at me like I had two heads. "I drink wine. That's it. I may have had too much today, but that's the fuck it is. Don't insult me like that. You know better."

I had to admit that she was right. But I wasn't about to let her off that easy.

"Monica, you need to slow down on that shit before you think about trying something else. I didn't marry a crackhead, and I'm not going to start this late in the game with you." I had to be straight with her. I loved her to death, but I had boundaries.

"You don't ever have to worry about that. That shit doesn't look good on me. I'm only addicted to you."

I had to admit that she made me smile on the inside. She knew what to say to make a man feel good. I'm just going to move on with my agenda. She was drunk in love. The way that I loved for her to be.

It didn't take long for my sex drive to return and to get her to do for me what I originally wanted her to do when I first came in the house.

We made out on that sofa like it was going out of style. She damn near sucked my tongue right out of my mouth with the passion that she had going on. She a straight beast, and I had to admit that she was giving me everything that she had. She got up and damn near ripped the pants right off me. Took my dick in her mouth and engulfed it like she was a magician and she was trying to make it disappear. She was doing a fabulous job of it. I prayed that Corey didn't come in because I wouldn't have stopped her finishing what she was doing for no one. I wouldn't have explained it to him anyway. I'm sure he is out there in the world knocking women off left and right. He's my boy, and the apple that fell from this tree didn't roll at all.

Before I knew it, I exploded in her mouth, and she took it all in stride. She wasn't finished, but it felt like I was. That nut took some energy from me. But that didn't stop her from demanding more.

"Let's go upstairs. I want to finish you off," she said seductively as she got up and pulled at my arm so that I would get up off the couch.

I did as she requested and unexpectedly picked her up as if she were a newborn baby and carried her up the stairs and to our bedroom. I laid her on the bed, and she quickly undressed and spread her legs for me like a butterfly's wings. She beckoned with a seductive flicker of her tongue across her top lip. I undressed and crawled across the bed and intensively went to work on her pussy as if there was no tomorrow. She grabbed my head and pushed me in deeper as she moaned uncontrollably.

"I'm coming," she moaned. I pulled back and watched her twitch as she exploded in an orgasm. It made me rock hard again.

"Now fuck the shit out of me. I want that dick in me. I want to feel you in me. Fuck me now." She rolled over on her stomach and arched her midsection into the air and waited for me to mount her and take her for a ride. I did what came natural and slid into her wet canal. She was tight and pulsating around my dick. It drove me crazy as I slowly pumped in and out of her. The connection that I was feeling with her took me back to when we were younger, and I loved it. We both climaxed again before collapsing beside each other. I was spent. I thought that she was, but I was mistaken. Before I could even speak again, Monica rolled over and began to suck on my dick again. She was blowing my mind. It took her a minute to get it hard once more, but when she did, she straddled me and rode me until I came again. I don't know what point she was trying to prove, but she was going for Wife of the Year. My wife was the winner and the only woman for me. She had no competition, and no other woman could even come close to her. My wife is my only chick, and I was very content with her.

Chapter 47

Monica

Different

I woke up this morning feeling like a piece of shit warmed over. I was hungover and didn't like it. I was in bed, and I didn't remember even getting there. My husband was still asleep beside me, which was rare, because the clock on my nightstand read 7:30 in the morning. Lately, he's been absent from the house by that time. He was snoring loud too.

I shifted in bed a few more minutes before I rolled on to my feet. As soon as I lifted myself from the bed, I became light-headed. I quickly reached for the nightstand while whispering the name of Jesus. After a few more seconds, I slowly walked to the bathroom to slap some water on my face and to relieve my bladder.

When I got to the bathroom and I flipped on the light switch, what stood before me in the mirror was someone that I didn't recognize. I looked tattered and worn. My eyes were red, and my hair needed to be combed.

I did my ritual as I usually did in the morning, but this time, I showered a little longer than I normally did. I felt dirty, and I didn't know why. When I finally stepped out of the shower, my husband greeted me with a towel and a smile. It was unusual for him to do that. Not that he wasn't caring, it was just something that he hasn't done in a long time.

"Good morning, bae," he said as he wrapped the towel around me, and then kissed me on the cheek.

I looked at him strangely as he did that, because, again, it wasn't the norm.

"Are you okay?" I asked him.

"Monica, I'm great. Why you ask me that?"

"Because this isn't normal for you. It's been a minute since you brought me a towel. It caught me off guard," I said as I took control of the towel and continued to dry myself off. I looked at him in the eyes while doing this. He looked innocent, to be truthful. But my mind instantly went back to the pictures and the bitch he had on the side, and I tightened my grip on the towel as I dried myself.

"Neither was last night. You put the pussy on a brother like when we were first dating. I mean, you knocked me out cold. I haven't slept that good in a long time." He was smiling from ear to ear. I was oblivious to the night before. I didn't remember the sex at all. I hope he wasn't expecting an encore performance because I didn't have it right now. Nor did I want to. I still felt like shit.

"I'm glad you enjoyed yourself." I put on a fake smile to hide the contempt I was feeling for him and myself. I pushed past him with newfound energy and made my way downstairs and toward the kitchen. I needed some coffee and to put something in my stomach. I'm sure that the rest of the house would be hungry as well.

I was a mother, wife, and daughter. But more than anything, I was a woman. A woman who pushed past how she felt and did what she needed to do to keep her family together, and that meant doing it despite what it looked like or how I felt.

"Ma, you okay?" Corey asked as he sat down at the table and I brought him his breakfast.

"Yes, why do you ask?" I mainly asked to see if he could read past my present façade.

"You just look different. I don't know."

"Well, I did overdo it yesterday, and now, I'm feeling the effects of it. I'm just a bit tired. As soon as I get some food and coffee in me, I'll be just fine." I smiled afterward to give him the impression that I believed in what I just stated. But, truthfully, I didn't know what was going to make me feel any better. I felt like shit. I felt different. It didn't help that my husband looked at me with lust in his eyes as he ate. I don't know what the hell I did to him last night, but he must have loved it. A piece of me hoped that he enjoyed it enough to leave his side piece alone. I felt like I was losing my grip on me *and* him. I felt different.

Chapter 48

Corey

Give and Take

They say that a relationship is about give and take, and I think that Dre and I had it down to a science. Sexually and mentally, we were doing the damn thing. Like right now, we were out touring all the trap houses my father had set up around the city and meeting with all my father's lieutenants. My father put me under Dre's care and guidance for a great deal of my training. My father still put in his time, but with him doing what he needed to do to take over the rest of the city, he still needed to get me groomed to help at the table. I had to admit that I was in awe at how much it took to run a growing empire. This shit is work. I can see why my father was out all the time. He had tons of shit going on. Buyers, dealers, distributors, hit men, casers, and tons of other positions, and he had to keep all of that shit together.

After a full day of running around in the streets, of which he had me paying attention to hand gestures, crackhead tendencies, and all types of stuff that a normal person would miss daily, we headed to a drive-thru restaurant and grabbed a quick bite to eat. I had to say that I was growing quite comfortable with Dre's presence in my life. He was a great teacher and very patient. I guess that came with age, which we never talked about.

"Do you have a problem fucking someone under the legal age limit?"

"No" was the only word that came out of his mouth. I still getting used to questions being answered in the manner that they were supposed to be answered. Many people want to explain themselves in a simple question, which, for the most part, isn't necessary.

"Explain," I requested. We were both in the car eating our meal, and there was silence, as usual.

"Age limit laws were created by men and a broken system. How can one group of people tell another group what is appropriate? In this case, I know that I'm dealing with a person underage by law but very competent in decision-making skills. In layman's terms, you man enough to handle this." He continued to eat his food after he said what he had to say as if it wasn't some profound shit. That shit turned me the fuck on. I wanted to eat his ass like he was eating that hamburger right now.

"That's some real shit right there," I nodded my head. The nasty thoughts were still on my mind, but I didn't want lust to control me and have me lose my focus.

"So what are we doing here? I mean, is this what some would call a relationship?" I guess I wanted to have someone in my corner in word and deed besides my immediate family. Most people wanted companionship.

"This is give and take. No lovers, boyfriends, or partners. I don't like labels. Let's keep it cool. I got your back, and you got my back. Simple."

"Cool." I nodded my head once again.

We finished our food and then sat in silence a bit.

I unzipped my pants and pulled out my dick. I reclined my chair and began to jerk myself until I got hard. Dre was always game for sex, so he bent over into my position and took me into his mouth. I enjoyed the way he gave head. There was some experience behind the way he used his tongue, and I loved it. This give-and-take thing we had going on was simple.

As he bobbed up and down on my dick, I reached behind him and pushed my hands down the back of his pants. He pulled his pants down in the process of continuing to give me head. I loved it. He pulled himself up on his knees to give me more access to his hole, which I fingered feverishly. Dre wasn't a moaner, but he let me know that he was liking it when the intensity of his blow job went up a notch. He had my toes curling in my shoes. I loved it. It didn't take long before I strapped a Magnum condom on and pushed my dick deep into his ass. We were in a secluded area of the city, so I took my time and fucked him slow and easy. Some may say we were making love, but I digress. This was me giving and him taking.

Chapter 49

Clayton

For Better or Worse

I looked over at my husband with confusion on the inside but a bright smile on the outside. It was threatening to fall into a frown. I was doing my best to hold it together. I wanted to yell out "Who the fuck are you?" but I didn't. Everything he did right now made me crazy. It had only been a few hours since I discovered the symbols from my case in his office and a few other places around the house. I wanted to get out of the house and get down to my office to do some research, but I didn't want to blow anything or jump the gun. I could be wrong about all of this . . . or I could be sleeping with the enemy.

"Babe, what's wrong with you? You've been preoccupied ever since I got home. Did you enjoy your time off from work?" We were both sitting at the dining-room table enjoying a meal.

"Well, I have enjoyed it for the most part, but I can't wait to get back to work. I have some leads that look promising," I said and put a spoonful of food in my mouth that I cooked before he got home. I was trying my best to not play my hand. Even though I don't know what his function may be in this case, I didn't want to say anything that would blow it.

"That's great. I really hope you get these scumbags off the street so I won't have to treat any more of these addicts." He looked and sounded convincing when he talked, but I was not believing him much. Everything he said and did was suspect now.

"So how was your day?" I asked, changing the subject a bit.

"It was nothing but sick people all day. You know, the usual. So boring."

"I thought that you loved your job?" I asked, probing him. I was hoping that he gave up some type of information without being aware. I tried to put on a jovial and upbeat façade to mask my probe.

"I do love my job, but it does get boring at times. You know, a rut." Again, he looked sincere in his speaking, but I felt like he wanted to open up some more.

"So is this your dream job? Or something your parents persuaded you to do?" I knew that I had asked him this type of question before, but I wanted to see if I would get something different today.

"Well, I always wanted to be in the medical field. I just didn't know what I wanted to do."

"So, what field would have made you happy all of the time if you had a choice?"

"I really wanted to make people beautiful, but my parents told me that cosmetic surgery was for freaks and that the doctors were freaks to do that to people, so I crossed that off my list and went into internal medicine." He seemed a little glum as he said that statement, like it was the truth and he was speaking from a painful place in his life.

"Wow. That's amazing. I'm sure that you would have been a wonderful surgeon." I reached over and placed my hand on top of his hand that was resting on the table. I still had some genuine feelings for him. I was just hoping that I was wrong about all of this, and it was just a huge coincidence with the Chinese symbols in his house and on the dead bodies.

"So are you any closer to finding the drug dealers that you're on the lookout for?"

"Well, I have some promising leads that have fell in my lap. I hope that they lead to my persons of interest."

"These drug dealers can be so elusive at times. Is that something that bothers you?" he looked at me intently. His question seemed like it had a bit of provoking in it. But I could be wrong. It could be my frustrations and confusion getting the best of me.

"No, not really. It's all about timing and patience. As the saying goes, 'every dog has its day.'" I smiled. I just didn't know why.

"I have to say that I agree with you. And I can't wait until that day to be by your side when you get your dog." He smiled too. But it made me a little nervous.

Chapter 50

Avery

Wanted

I was in my bed for once with my eyes closed. I wasn't sleeping, I was resting my mind. It was constantly going, and I needed a break. My phone broke me out of my concentrative state.

I rolled over and retrieved my personal phone from its charging spot. I looked at the phone to see that it was Monica. A smile spread across my face. She wanted a hit. I loved being her secret supplier without her knowledge.

"Good day, Monica."

"How are you doing, Coach?"

"I'm thriving in the land of the living. You?"

"I'm doing great. I'm calling you to see if you would like to come to my house for dinner. My husband wanted to thank you for being a stand-up guy with our son."

"Oh really?" I was shocked. I had got something wrong. She didn't want any wine. Her husband wanted to size me up in person. I'm sure she talks about me and the things that we have done together. I'm also sure she left out the fact that one of my friends was gay. He would have none of that, I'm positive.

"You sound surprised."

"I'm not surprised, per se. I don't get many invites to homes of the young men that I train in basketball. It's an honor." The lies were flowing effortlessly. I loved it.

"My husband is an honorable man, and he gives people their props when it's due. Your contribution to our son's life is great, and we want to thank you for it. Any positive addition to his life should be rewarded." I can see that she was still playing the devoted wife to the core. I'll give her points for playing her position, even though it will be her downfall.

"I'm honored. I'll be there. I just need to know the time and address again."

"I'll text you it after we get off the phone. Oh, and I would like to meet your wife. Bring her too." She hung up the phone without giving me a chance to answer.

"This bitch." I wasn't expecting her to ask to see my imaginary wife. I was going to make up a good excuse about why she couldn't come when I get there.

Even though I had all the information already, I went with the flow and texted her back that I got it and would be looking forward to getting to know the "wonderful" family that has trained such an ambitious young man. I didn't mention "my wife," because, like I said before, I would give an excuse for her absence when I got to the house. This made me wonder if Monica was as naïve as I perceived her to be. We will see.

This was a monumental moment for me because I was going into the home of a person that wanted me dead. He didn't know that I was molding his son to join my ranks. I was going to use his son to learn his practices, and then take it all from him. It wasn't what I was going to do, it was *how* I was going to do it. I didn't want to drag Corey out of the closet, but it was the only way that I was going to get him to side with me. I was his real family anyway. The world and his father wanted no part of him and his sexuality, so I was going to do it for him. That is what a real father does anyway. They strip you down before the world does it. I did it to myself and built a great empire in the process.

I wanted to look good for this event. I got up out of my bed and went to find some attire that would go well with the event.

I dressed and made my way to the home of my enemy, protégé, and customer. I drove a car that a coach and civilian with little finances would drive, a KIA. I wanted to give the impression that I didn't have much money and that they were doing me a favor by inviting me to their home.

I pulled up to the house and admired it for a few seconds. I had to admit that it was a nice house and in a decent, middle-class neighborhood. The house was a detached two story with a garage and manicured lawn. Flower beds were spread across the front of the house, along with a very nice stone-paved walkway. There were no fancy cars outside and nothing outlandish to indicate the way that Leroy was making his money. At least he had some smarts in that area.

I exited the car and walked up the short walkway, rang the doorbell, and Corey answered with a smile on his face.

"Hey, Coach. Welcome to our home." He stepped back and allowed me to walk in. A smile came on my face when I entered the small foyer and marveled at the great décor that was spread out on the walls and the room that housed the stairway upstairs and the few doors that surrounded it. It was classy and well put together.

"I'm so glad that you like our home," Monica said as she and Leroy walked into the room that we were in.

"This is very well put together," I said as I reached out to shake Leroy's hand.

"My wife is a beast with the décor. I sprinkled some things in too, but this home is financed by me and run by her."

"This is so nice to hear." His ego was at work like he had the perfect family or something. I can put some cards on the table that would cave in his chest and have him tucking his ego in his ass. "It's not common in this day and age to have a well set up and run family setting. I admire it greatly."

Leroy smiled with the pride that he should have even though he was living a lie that he would soon find out about.

"Come into the dining room, fellas, and get seated. Dinner will be ready shortly." We all followed instructions and made our way into the dining room. That too was nice. I was impressed once again with the décor in that room as well. Nothing flashy or extravagant like you see on those shows that feature homes of the rich and famous. I knew that Leroy was making money in the streets and enough to live better than this. He just didn't flaunt it. That was admirable of him. I was making more than he and knew the traps of exposing one's self to looking and living recklessly just because you have finances to do so.

We sat in silence before the conversation was started up again by Leroy.

Chapter 51

Leroy

Table for Two

"How long have you been coaching?" I asked my son's coach. I was asking because my son and the team he was on was having a fantastic season. I was impressed with the way that Corey was responding to him. Corey was a loner by nature, and I haven't seen him with any friends like most boys his age. Now that he was on this team, he was more upbeat. He wasn't depressed or anything like that, and he has been playing sports for a while now. It's just a different response from him when he started playing basketball with this team, and even he developed a friendship with Dre. This guy is teaching Corey how to be a team player and a leader, and I'm grateful for it. I didn't need help raising my son, but the way Corey talks about this guy and the way that I have seen him direct the team call for me to give props where it's due.

"I've been coaching for about ten years now."

"Coach, or can I call you Clarence?"

"Clarence is fine."

"Clarence, I want to thank you for displaying great leadership in front of my son and trusting him in a leadership position." I didn't compliment men that often, but in this instance, it was necessary.

"It's easy to do with someone so great to work with." He looked at me, and then at my son. I felt proud to receive the good news that I trained my son well.

"Do you have any children?" He was someone who was good with children, so I assumed he had to have at least one.

"None biologically, but I have many that I have sown into over the years." His smile was a little smug. He had some arrogance, but most men did.

"So, what do you do for a living? If you don't mind me asking," Corey's coach asked me.

"Well, I manage the supplying of a plethora of agents to people that help them escape reality," I answered as aptly as I knew how. A drug kingpin just sounds rather boring.

"A street pharmacist?" he smiled.

"You can call it that too," I smiled right back. It almost sounded like he was making fun of me or shaming me. I instantly caught an attitude and positioned myself straight up in the chair, looking him straight in the eyes. Man-to-man. For all I know he could be an undercover cop positioned to take me down.

"There is no shame in suppling a need. A man making a living for himself and the ones he loves is very admirable and off-limits to judgement in my book. No matter what it is." He earned my trust back just that easy.

"I appreciate the honesty. It's real out here, and there's always another man trying to hinder your come up. Like this gay muthafucka that is pissing in my water, so to speak. This faggot is hiding in the closet and won't show his muthafuckin' face like a real man would. But he'll have his day. It's coming to an end. Best believe that." Just thinking about it made me pissed off.

"Tell 'em how you really feel, why don't ya?" Coach said, and then laughed afterward. It did cause a smile to spread across my face. This guy was a class act in my book.

"Sorry, I didn't mean to lay my problems on the table. It's just a man problem, you know."

"I know all about it." He nodded his head. "We all have our enemies."

"Coach, I think I'm a good judge of character, and I have not been around you much, but I get the vibe that you are a good guy trying to do good things in the lives of young black men. I commend that. I just don't see you as having enemies. Plus, my wife and son speak so highly of you.

"I could actually use someone on my team like you. But something tells me that's not the type of business that you want to get involved with." He looked and sounded respectable, but it could have been a front.

"You are correct. No disrespect. I like to stay in my lane."

"I understand that and hope that my business and dealings remain in the confines of your mind." I didn't want it to come off threatening, but I was serious about what I just spoke.

"No problem. Your secret is safe with me. I wouldn't dare speak a word of your business. I love the lane I'm in, and I appreciate it when others do the same. It's all about appreciation and respect. Can't have one without the other." Clarence nodded his head, and he kept his eyes on mine. Which was a sign of respect and agreement.

"It's cool to have another man of honor sitting across the table from me."

"I would agree with that as well. It's a rare thing to see and do nowadays. There is so much backstabbing going on in the world. You can hardly trust anyone anymore." He was speaking nothing but the truth.

"Man, there is a strong trust factor going on with this gay faction of drug dealers and criminals. Them ass fuckers are loyal to this ghost guy for sure. It's some crazy shit. I don't understand it."

"Well, some things are just not meant to be understood."
He had a smirk on his face that gave me pause. There was
something about it that just didn't sit right with me. I'm
going to have Dre do some research on this brother. I got
to see who's sitting at my table right now for sure.

Chapter 52

Monica

Like a Leaf

It felt like the dead of winter in my room, but I was sweating like a pig. I had been in my bed for hours. I had to detox myself off the wine that I was drinking like a fish in water. I knew that I had a problem when I called the coach at like five in the morning for a bottle of wine the other day. I wanted to have some with my lunch and dinner. It seemed like I couldn't get through the day without it. I knew this was the sign of an addict. I didn't think that I could or would be addicted to anything in my life. I knew that my husband had my attention, but now this damn wine was taking over too.

There was a knock on my door.

"Come in," I yelled out. My son, Corey, peeked his head in, and then the rest of him followed. He came in and got a good look at me. My hair was all over my head, and I'm sure my face looked flushed. He looked at me in pity as he sat on the bed with me.

"Wow, Ma, you sick?" he asked.

"Yeah, I think so." I am not going into details with him about the wine and all of that. It's none of his business, and I don't want him all in my business anyway. He is way too protective of me, and I don't want to be smothered or micromanaged by a teenager.

"You look rough. I need to get away from you," he laughed. I laughed and followed it with a fake cough to give him the impression that I was sick with a cold and not otherwise.

"Yeah, you may be right." I threw in another cough for good measure.

"If I didn't know any better, you look like you coming down from a high like one of those drug addicts I've seen with Dad and Dre on the streets."

I didn't say anything for a moment because it had stunned me. I was ashamed. Deeply ashamed.

"Speaking of drugs, how is the training going with your father? Is it all that you thought it would be? Are you sure that's what you want to do? Are you afraid?"

"Wow, that's a lot of questions at one time. Did you take a breath?" He laughed again. I was glad to see him in good spirits. The drug game can suck the life out of you and leave you with no emotions.

"I know. It's just that I'm worried about you becoming your father. I want you to make decisions for yourself and not to please us. We love you, but we won't be here for you forever. Everything has an expiration date."

"Dang, why you getting all mushy?" He looked uncomfortable like many men did when it came to death and emotional things.

"I'm not emotional or mushy. These streets are treacherous and not for the faint of heart. You got to be strong and make some hard decisions. I want you to be sure you're in this. It's almost always no backing out once you're in. I come from a long line of drug dealers, and I married one, so it comes from experience, not emotions. I'm telling you to be about your shit if you going to do it."

He sat there on the edge of my bed very quiet for a few seconds. I knew that he was processing all that I just said to him. I knew that he could handle it. I just wanted him to be sure of his own choices and not ones someone else gives or influences.

"Ma, I got this. I'm my father's son, and I'm my own man. I know that this will not be easy, and I will be on the lookout, like you always taught me. I got this, and I got you. So back to you. I'm about to go do this game in about an hour, but I'll hook you up with some care before I leave."

"Okay," I nodded my head in agreement.

The mention of the game led to me thinking about the coach; then that led to me thinking about the wine.

"While you're out, could you see if Coach has some more of that wine he gave me a few weeks back? It was very nice tasting." I hate lying to my son because I just got a bottle from Coach a day ago, but he knew nothing about it. And that was on top of the bottle that he brought when he came over for dinner the other day.

"You sure about that? Because I'm sure wine don't cure a cold." He looked at me with a smirk on his face.

"Neither does minding my business, but you are doing that oh so well, aren't you," I gave a smile. He laughed again.

"Cool, Ma, I got you." He walked out of the room. Shame enveloped me for a moment; then the thought of the wine being in my hand and the taste of it going down diminished the shame.

Chapter 53

Corey

Premonitions

"The choice is yours," I heard my father speak. His voice sounded louder than normal, and it echoed throughout the room that we were in. I looked at him in his eyes and knew that he was serious. Very serious. I looked over at Dre, and my heart sank. His hands and legs were tied to a wooden chair. We were in the small room with two of my father's men standing in two corners of the room with my father in the middle close to Dre. I was against a wall with my body positioned toward them and the only door to the room. There was only one sound in the room that I heard, and that was the beat of my own heart. I was speechless. I didn't think that I would ever get caught. Now, here we are. I sat freely, unlike Dre. My father paced around Dre with a gun in his hand. All I could think about was the worst thing possible. Dre dying right in front of me.

"I can't believe that my own flesh and blood was a dick and ass chaser. Here I am doing all that I can to provide for you and your mother, and this is what I get as a reward. A fucking faggot. You had me fooled." He slapped Dre in the head with the gun, causing blood to splatter and run down his face. Dre didn't show any signs of weakness, though. He didn't budge at all. He looked at my father in the eyes the whole time. There was no sweat covering his face. No trembling or any such thing. He was the soldier that he portrays himself to be.

"And this was the piece of shit that you were sleeping with the whole time underneath my nose. You were supposed to be my right-hand man, and here you are dicking down my son, my own flesh and blood. You had me fooled. You had us all fooled. You all were fucking like rabbits, and then sitting at this table like all was right in the world. The ultimate betrayal in my book. I'm looking for a gay drug dealer with two right in my face." He then spat in my face. The hate was real on his face. I was no longer his son right now.

"As I said before, the choice is yours. You're going to choose your boyfriend's fate. A slow death or a quick one?" He looked at me, and then at Dre. Chills went down my spine. But I didn't show the hurt that I felt on the inside.

He then walked away from me and over to the table where a cooler was sitting on top of it. My mind raced with curiosity of what was in the cooler. It seemed like it took him forever to open the top to reveal what was inside.

"Here, we have slow death." He held up what looked like a syringe with blood in it. "This is a fresh dose of slow death or what is known to most as HIV."

My heart sank once again.

"Now, how do you want your boyfriend to die? His death is in your hands."

My eyes shot open, and I sat up in bed. I was happy to realize that I had just had a dream. I hope that it wasn't a premonition or something like that. Dre and I have been discreet, but you never know what is going on in the drug world until it is up on you. I can't put anything past my father for obvious reasons. I needed to get me a decoy. I need a girlfriend. I don't even know if I would or could play the role of a boyfriend to a girl. I guess I would just have to go and find out. I had a girl that was interested in me, and she was pretty enough to choose her as a candidate. The only problem I had to figure out is how much I wanted her to know. I think it's best that she thinks that I am totally into her and not let her know that she is being used. It's not a nice thing to do to a person, but life is about taking chances. She would be taking a chance, and I would take a chance as well. I would be sure to make it worth her while, however. She looked like she'd be a good whore or thot anyway.

I didn't have practice or experience with a girl, but I saw what my father did with my mother, and I'm sure I could do the same. I just hope I did a good job with it.

I decided to get dressed and drive to her house to get the ball rolling. I didn't have time to play games. She was going to be my girl from jump.

I had on my best street/hood boy attire because I knew that is what she liked from seeing her in school and the boys she dated. I usually dressed with clothes that fit me and not hang off my butt. My parents, mainly my mother, told me to dress presentable always. She said even though we were a family that was "street active," we didn't want to be perceived as such. So now my pants were sagging off my butt, and I had my shirt untucked and a fitted baseball hat on that screamed: "about that life."

I would have to break her in and give her the speech. She was mine from here until I release her.

I walked up to her door and rang the bell. I was a bit nervous, but I put on an act and rode this thing out.

"Can I help you?" Her father opened the door and looked me up and down. It was expected.

"Is Diana home?" I looked him in his eyes, letting him know that I was serious and about my business.

"What's this about?" he asked. He was one of those professional and stern-looking fathers. He had on a suit and tie. His face was shaved and shaped up good. His voice was deep and firm. He was trying to intimidate me with questions and his stance in the doorway, but I was on a mission.

"She was supposed to be helping with some of my college applications." I was about to be in my last year of high school anyway, so that was a good lie, and it was credible. Diana was into the books and the thug boys. She wasn't a dummy when it came to books.

He looked me up and down for a few seconds and then closed the door in my face. I should have pushed in past him like I wanted to do, but I kept it cool and let this shit flow. I let him have the perception of being in control, but I knew that I was.

Diana appeared at the door moments later. She closed the door behind her slightly and stepped down onto the stoop and closer to me. She had a big butt and a nice pair of breasts to go with it. No weave or track in sight, but she could be sporting it, and I just don't know about it. It didn't make any difference to me, though. She was just a showpiece. I was going on my father's preference and what I hear other guys talk about most. I wasn't attracted to that stuff at all.

"Hey, wassup?" She had a smile on her face. She was an attractive girl, and I could see her on my arm for show.

"I wanted to take you out, but I wanted to surprise you." I licked my lips like I was LL Cool J. Her smile grew even wider after I did that. I knew I had her.

"Really?"

"I been digging you for a minute, but I wasn't ready for a girl of your caliber yet." I yeasted that thing up knowing that she would take it all in. I didn't take her as being desperate, but she probably wanted to hear stuff like that. Most women did. "I'm ready for you."

"Wow, that's so sweet."

"Yeah, so are you, I'm sure. Get yourself together and I'll scoop you up in about twenty minutes. We going out wherever you want to go."

"It's like that?" She looked at me in surprise. I couldn't blame her. I would have been surprised too.

"Of course. You're mine now."

I walked away feeling in charge and was liking the growth and confidence that came with power. I liked power. No, I *loved* it.

Chapter 54

Clayton

Magnum Mouth

I palmed the back of his head like it was a basketball. He was going up and down on my dick like he was a pro. Shit, he *was* a pro. My dick fit in his mouth like a Magnum condom on a big dick. He was truly a "Magnum mouth" for sure. He was giving it so good that it caused my pelvis to rise from the edge of the bed I was sitting on and pump his face like I wanted to do his ass shortly. I was on the verge of busting when I pulled back and softly pushed him away.

"All fours," were the instructions I gave him. He looked at me with lust in his eyes as he followed the instructions I gave him. I too gave him "the look" as he made his way onto the canopy bed that we started to share not too long ago.

I eased onto the bed and positioned myself behind him, prepped to take full advantage of his wet hole. I reached over his body and pushed his upper body closer to the bed, simultaneously putting his ass in position for a pounding. We had made love before, but now it was just time for some good old-fashioned fucking.

I griped my dick and pushed it into the hole that was waiting for me.

"Uhnnn," Anthony grunted as I plunged into him with my whole girth. He was wet, which caused the air to be filled with a sloshing sound. I loved that sound as I went in and out of him with aggression. I was mad at him for being the one and not being the one at the same time. I had done some research on him and what I discovered was not easy to read or comprehend. It broke my heart. I was fucking him with intentions of breaking his heart like he did mine. I was trying to fuck a hole in his heart.

Earlier that day, I was in my office all day like a hermit crab. I contacted the IRS about a copy of his last tax return and was surprised by the earnings that he was making. Then I looked up the cost of his house and found out that he couldn't possibly be paying for that house he had on his salary as a doctor. He was doing something on the side. But *what* was the question.

A few days ago, I hired a private investigator to track down his school history. Come to find out he had a cosmetic surgery office in Atlanta that he closed a few years ago under an investigation into his practices and moved here to Baltimore.

All this was very suspicious but not hard-core evidence.

I called in a favor and got a copy of his phone record for the last few months and sifted through his call log to see who he was calling and who he was calling the most. There were a few numbers that stood out, but I had someone else work on them to get me some rock-solid evidence.

I scanned in my head our celebration party trying to see if anyone there looked or acted suspicious so that I could get their name from Anthony. I was fishing for anything to prove myself wrong. But it wasn't adding up that way. With each new discovery, I had grown angrier and angrier. Angry at him for deceiving me, and me for falling for it so easily. I was supposed to be smarter and more alert.

I was brought back to the present with the moans of Anthony beneath me.

"Damn, baby, you're wearing me out." He thrust back toward me with aggression and passion. We were grinding our bodies together causing friction. It, combined with the friction going on in my head, was driving me insane. It caused me to thrust harder until I climaxed; then I fell on top of him.

I could feel my heartbeat against his back as I lay there in exhaustion. It felt like it was about to burst. I finally rolled off him and collapsed on my back next to him.

I lay there in silence with so much swirling in my head.

"Baby, what got into you?" he said as he snuggled up against me. His touch almost made me cringe, but I held it together. "You worked me over so good that I don't even want to move."

"I don't know. I couldn't resist myself." I smiled, but it was all fake. My love for him was fading fast.

"I'm so in love with you. I'm so glad that I found you. You saved my life." His hand moved all over my chest.

"Let me get in the shower and rinse myself off." I quickly got up and headed out of the room and into the bathroom within seconds. I locked the door behind me so he couldn't get in the shower with me. I turned the shower on and then hopped in. I heard Anthony knocking on the door, but I ignored it. He went away after a few minutes. A part of me wanted to let him join me, but that wasn't something that I wanted to do right now. I just slept with who may be my enemy and my come up. Maybe I was looking at this the wrong way. Maybe I should just play this thing out until more solid evidence came about.

I was in the bathroom for about twenty minutes before I made my exit.

I walked into the bedroom with a towel. He was sitting on the bed when I walked in. He had a sullen look on his face which caused me to question him.

"Baby, what's wrong?" I asked as I sat down beside him.

"Why did you lock the door to the bathroom?"

"I used the toilet before I took the shower, and I didn't want you to be uncomfortable with the smell. I think that's rude."

"I should have known that was the reason. I thought that I did something wrong." He had on a very sweet face that caused me to melt.

"No, that's just one of my pet peeves," I said as I kissed him on the cheek.

"I guess I must get to know you more so I know what you like and don't like."

"Yes, we do have to get to know each other better."

"So can your husband get a little snack before bed? I'm a slight bit famished."

"Oh, you are, are you?" He smiled.

"Yes, I used a ton of energy, and I need fuel just in case I need to have a second round." When he got up, I swatted him on the butt for good measure. I was going to be a good actor until all the pieces come together. At least I would be getting some good ass until my time is up. Free ass is always a plus. It's a pity that I'll have to start over again in the love game.

Anthony returned with a hearty bowl of fruit and cheese to help me get my energy back up. It didn't take long to mount my husband to get me what may be my last nut from him.

Chapter 55

Avery

Closets

I grew impatient, and I was about to push my plan full steam ahead. It was time to wrap this game up and move in for the checkmate. We were on the last two games of the season, and we were poised to take the championship. I wanted the whole city as well. That is what I was getting ready to do.

We had just wrapped up another game with a win, and I was sitting in my office taking a breather. I was waiting for Corey to join me in the office. I was about to inform him that he was now working for me while he was working for his dad.

There was a knock on the door.

"Come in," I answered.

Corey came in dressed in his street clothes. I had to say that he was a very good-looking young man. He favored his mother more than his father.

"Corey, do you know why I called you here?" Of course, he didn't know. I just wanted to see where his head was at.

"No, sir. But I'm sure that you're going to tell me," he smiled. It was a bright and youthful smile. I remember having one a long time ago. It has since been long gone. His will fade soon too. I'm sure of it.

"Good answer. Corey, there is one thing about people that really irks me to the core."

"What's that, Coach?" he asked. He looked like he was hanging on to my every word.

"Secrets. I don't like secrets. Especially being hidden from me."

He was quiet. I guess he didn't know what I was talking about.

"Do you have any secrets, Corey?"

"None that I can think of." He looked at me straight in the eyes. He didn't flinch at all. He was a great liar. Too bad I was going to have to burst his bubble.

"You don't have any secrets? None?" I gave him another opportunity to confess. I know that there was pressure to keep a certain persona in the public eye and keep your manliness at the forefront always. I wasn't mad at it at all. Especially because it helped me rule and roam undetected for so long. They, the world and its standard of manhood, gave me the key to pillage the land that they walked in so freely.

"No secrets." He kept his cool about him and continued his stance. It was why I wanted him on my team.

"So when were you going to come out of the closet?"

"What closet? Ain't no closets in here," he said, playing dumb, and then began to laugh.

"You know what I'm talking about. No one knows that you love dick and ass."

"Yes, I'm in love with my dick and my ass. Shit, I love all of me." He was not going to come out and say it, so I had to pull out the ammunition I had in the gun.

I reached in the drawer to my desk and pulled out an envelope that favored the one that I gave his mother awhile ago. I slid it across the desk and waited for him to open it.

He looked at it for a few seconds, and then looked at me.

"Who's that for?"

"Don't waste my damn time. Open the damn envelope!" I barked. He was being immature.

He took my seriousness to heart and pulled the envelope off the desk and opened it.

He took out the pictures that I had taken of him and Dre. They thought that they were being discreet and making sure that his father didn't catch them, but they were worried about the wrong person catching them. That was naïve on his part, but expected.

"You have anything you want to say to me?" I asked.

"So what the hell do you want from me? So you have some pictures of me having sex with a man. What do you want me do? Cry and ask for your help to get over this?" He looked at me with a sarcastic look on his face.

"No, I want you to know that I want you on my team."

"I'm already on the team."

"That's not the team I'm talking about. I'm the guy your father is looking for."

There was a silence on both of our ends. Mine because I wanted him to process what he just heard. I knew that it wasn't easy news to hear. Probably unbelievable. Shit, I played my hand well enough not to be believed. I wasn't perfect, just good at going off other people's perception. I play the part and do it well. Corey was good at it too. That's why I picked him, because we had things in common, mainly remaining anonymous. I'm assuming that he put so much energy into playing his role that he missed the signs from the others around him.

"You're so funny," Corey started to laugh. My facial expression remained straight and unmoved by his laughter. This made him laugh even more.

"Corey, this is no joke. I'm dead serious." I leaned in closer to him.

"Get the fuck out of here. No, the hell you are not." He looked at me in disbelief.

"Corey, I'm the Ghost. I am just like you. I like men and all of my men like men."

"So you want me to believe that you like men?"

"Corey, I have no reason whatsoever to lie to a teenager about anything. I'm telling you that is who the fuck I am, and I'm not going to explain it."

"Man, I have to say that I'm blown away." Corey sat back in the chair that he was in and a smile came across his face.

"What's the smile on your face for?"

"I have a secret and you have one. We're even."

"Corey, there is one problem with your math. We are *never* even. I am, and will always be, above you. If you want your secret to stay safe with me, then I need all the information on your father's operation, and I won't be forced to let him know about his son and his lover, and I am not talking about that pretty chick you have been parading around. She's a good touch, though, I might add, but I will kill them all, and then you, if I even think that you are trying to out me. I'm sure your father has talked to you about my wrath. I will have no problem killing everyone close to you and letting you watch."

He looked on with not one word coming out of his mouth. In fact, Corey's mouth hung open in shock. He didn't even blink.

"Do we have an understanding?"

He nodded his head in agreement.

"I love you, unlike the world. They will never understand or care about the plight of a gay black man. Even your family. When you are gay, no one is loyal. No one.

"So keep me happy, and it will keep your family and friends alive. Got it?"

"Yes, sir," he answered.

"I don't want you to be afraid of me, but I do want you to fear me. There's a difference. You'll grow to learn the difference."

Chapter 56

Leroy

Choices

Corey and I were sitting in a car watching some of my
workers work. It was very low-key and calm. Corey had
to learn the traits of an addict to get fresh new ideas to
supply them and be with me in my meetings to know how
to govern the men and the money. I didn't want him to
think that it was easy at all. I wanted him to know that
his life was on the line every day, all day. There was a
moment of silence that came before this question. "Dad,
do you love me unconditionally?"

"Son, you already know that." I looked at him. "Where
is this question coming from?"

"Nowhere in particular. I just don't hear you say it.
That's all."

"Corey, I'm out in these streets fighting and scratching
to make a living for you every day, all day. I think that's
proof enough that I love you. I put my life on the line for
you and your mom all the time. You all are the reason I
grind so hard. I want the best for my family."

"That's cool, Pop. I appreciate that."

"I'm hoping that you will show me more than you tell,
as I do. Words are nothing without action behind them.
I want all men at my table. No punks allowed." I meant
what I said. Only the strong survive, and I believe that
with all that is within me.

Corey just nodded his head in agreement. There was silence once again. I enjoyed the bonding time that I was having with my son. I wanted this relationship with him. I was spending too much time in the streets and not enough time at home. The neglect was shown in the question he asked me. He thought I didn't love him. I had to admit that this was my fault by not rightly dividing my time between my family and the streets. This was my chance to make it right and bring my family back together, so we could take over this city together. Now it was my turn to ask a question and be proactive in my son's interests.

"Corey, what's up with that hot li'l mama you been bringing to the game? You got you a winner on your hands. She reminds me of your mama."

"Oh, Diana. She my girl. I just made it official recently because I wasn't sure of which way to go. Now I know, and she's going with me. She is hot too, Dad. She gives some mean head." Corey smiled as he was thinking about it. I knew that look all too well. His mama was a Magnum mouth herself.

It felt good to bond with my boy. He was right where I wanted him to be. A boy needs validation from his father, and I was going to make sure he got it from me.

"Corey, don't ever abuse or mistreat her. No matter what she does or says. Because women can be pistols and say some shit that will make you want to hurt them but just ignore it and move past it. Give her the attention she wants and needs. Gifts will never replace time spent, even if it not something you want to do. I've made that mistake a few times, and I'm still paying for it." I laughed at the end of my statement, but I meant it.

"I know." He nodded in response to my speech. He seemed like he was in a funk.

"Corey, I know you've seen me in some weird places and some crazy scenarios, but I want you to know that I love your mom, and I will never hurt her. These streets will take your mind if you let it, and for a moment, I was close to going crazy. But now that you're on board and learning quickly, I might add, this ghost guy don't know what's going to hit him. The Grant men are moving in for the kill." I don't know what was wrong with him, but I wanted to restore him in any area that he may be down in.

"So you ready for your last year of school?"

"Yeah." He didn't sound too convincing.

"Once you finish with that, you can completely focus on the family business and the takeover of the city. I want you to be a high school graduate. I didn't finish school, and I feel that it would make it easy for you to move up in life when high school is complete."

"Yeah, that sounds like a plan." He smiled. It was a weak one, though.

"Son, you seem like you have got a lot on your mind."

"Yeah, just life, though. Choices and life. That's all."

"Son, that is us all day long. Every person must make choices that will affect their tomorrow. We just don't know what tomorrow gonna hold. I say make investments that will secure your future, even if you not sure what's in the future. I'm making this money for the grandkids that I may or may not get to see. That's life."

"You make it sound so easy."

"Corey, life is one day at a time. I don't have an easy answer for you. It gets easier when you live day by day and invest in yourself. Do you believe in you?"

"Yes."

"Then that's all that matters. Fuck everyone else, even me and your mom. We can't make choices or live with those choices for you, so they damn well better be for you."

"Damn, it's like that." He looked at me like he was shocked that I said that. Even though I wanted my son to walk in my footsteps, I wasn't going to force him.

"Yes, it's like that. I must respect your choices, even if I don't like them. And that's what life is about: choices. They are free to make but may cost you a lot in the end." Even I was amazed by the last thing I said.

Corey looked at me in amazement. It was a look a father looked for to know that he has won over his son with trust and confidence.

Chapter 57

Monica

Fuck It

Patti LaBelle's "You Are My Friend" was playing on my surround sound as I lounged in the Jacuzzi tub all by myself. I was enjoying the wine that I copped from Coach once again. I had made up in my mind that I would stop when I wanted to. I was a fucking addict and liked it. Yes, I liked to nod the hell off to sleep from drinking the wine. It was taking more and more to get me lifted, but I didn't care. All I had to do was make a call or send a text to meet up with my connection. It was that simple.

I was in the house alone, and that was the norm nowadays since my husband and son were in the streets or at basketball games. I didn't even care, truth be told. I was in a fuck-it type of mood with the whole world for a while now. Everyone was doing them, and I am going to do the same.

I got up out of the tub and sauntered around the house in all my glory. I was naked, free, and loving it. I didn't care if my son walked in on me or not. He was the least of my worries.

My wine bottle was empty, and I was on the search for another bottle that I knew I had stashed around somewhere. I rummaged through a few cabinets before I found what I wanted. I sashayed back to sit in the tub and in my misery, once again. It amazed me how much energy it took to hold this family together and not focus on myself. It was the price that I paid for being a ride-or-die wife and mother. I lost myself in the shuffle, and now, I'm feeling the results of such.

I took the bottle of wine by the neck, threw my head back with it pressed against my lips, and took a long chug like the professional I was now. I relaxed in the tub and let the bottle in my hand hang over the side of the tub. I lay my head back and looked up to the ceiling. Tears flowed from my eyes and down the sides of my face. The truth was, I did care about my current condition. It just seemed like no one else did. The ones that were supposed to be paying attention to me were doing what they felt was best for them, and I was on the back burner.

"Why me, God?" I shook the bottle toward the sky. "Who going to take care of me? I took care of them for all this time. It's my time now. It's my time."

I felt the effects of the wine kicking in and the pain in my heart and mind easing its way out temporarily. I completely relaxed and let the cares of my world slip away as I relinquished my body to my temporary fix.

Chapter 58

Corey

Trust Issues

They say family is all that you have, and I believe that . . . to a degree. My father said that he loves me unconditionally, but that could change if my secret gets out. I think that he would not understand that I like men. Even if it is his son. Who could hate their own flesh and blood because of something as trivial as being gay? I think understanding will go out the window if he ever finds out. Everyone has a limit or a deal breaker. Was that the one that my father would have with me that would end his relationship with me? I was born into his life by his choice to sleep with Mom. Now I must deal with this shit that I didn't even ask for. And to add on top of that, a man that my father hates and I admire is gay and using me to get his agenda fulfilled. Talk about being fucked with no Astroglide. I can't trust either of them.

My mother was on some weird stuff lately. Her drinking was becoming a problem for me to deal with. Today, I got home early from a full day of the Drug Game 101 with my father, fake dating game with Diana, and going out with Dre on the low. I was exhausted, but all of it was fulfilling, though.

I walked into the house with the sound of music playing. I knew that it wasn't my father because he just didn't roll like that. I can't ever remember a time when I came home and he was listening to music. In the car, yes, but never at home. It could only be my mother. I was not in the mood to engage her or anyone else now, so I ignored the music and went up to my room. I was exhausted and just wanted to get some sleep. I'll deal with her in the morning or later. I'm sure she'll be up to check on me like she usually does. She was a consummate nurturer. She'll be fine until later.

I awoke to the noise of sirens; then my father rushed in my room.

"How the fuck are you up in here asleep and your mother down in the tub unconscious?" He looked at me like he wanted to kill me.

"What?" I shot up in the bed like one of those punching clowns that keep coming back at you. "Unconscious?"

"Yes, that's what the fuck I said." He left the room and rushed back down the stairs. I followed suit, seeing my mother in the middle of the floor stark naked. My father went back over to her in a panic.

"Monica . . . Monica . . . Wake up, baby . . . Wake up." I saw tears in my father's eyes as he cradled my mom's head. She was not responding. Her eyes were open. I looked on in fear and shock. I was stuck on stupid. I wanted to move, but I couldn't. The paramedics rushed in and took over, and before we knew it, they had my mother on a gurney and rushed her out of the house. My father hopped in the back of the ambulance, and I drove behind in the car.

As soon as we hit the hospital, I parked the car and made my way inside to see what was up. My heart was racing, and all types of things were going across my mind . . . mainly death. What if I lose my mother? How will I go on? How can I live?

"Dad, what's going on? Is she okay?" I rushed up to him as he was standing at a counter with a broken countenance. My father wasn't the mushy type and seeing him like this was new.

"They not telling me shit. They just took her to the back. I ready to blow this shit up if I don't get answers."

"Dad, I didn't know. I was tired, and I thought that she was just chilling like she's been. I didn't think it was . . . she was like . . ." I felt like my heart was breaking, and I didn't like it. I didn't like having no control over a situation.

It wasn't long before Dre came through the door and greeted my father as we were standing near the double doors that I assumed led to the back of the hospital. He glanced my way to acknowledge me, and I knew that he would address me later. My father was his boss, and I was something else. Something my father wouldn't understand or wanted to.

It was too much for me to care about that right now. It was on the back burner. I was in a new place with that too.

My father and Dre talked in a hushed tone, and it didn't take long for Dre to take charge and go to the counter, and then come back to my father near the double doors. I was sitting down in a chair not too far from them for a moment because I was going over in my mind about what I should or could have done to prevent this from happening. A few tears fell, and I didn't want my father or Dre to see me in a weak moment. Not long after, a doctor came out of the double doors. He walked over to my father and Dre. I hurried over to them with nervous anticipation. I wanted to see what was up—but I didn't either. I was crazy right now.

"Your wife is not responding." I walked up as the doctor started talking. "We're still running tests to see if we can pin-point what's going on. She was submerged underwater for quite awhile. It doesn't look good."

"What the hell do you mean?" my father said in anger.

"With cases like these, the outcome doesn't look promising. The brain requires oxygen, and if it goes without for a period of time, then things happen that may be irreversible."

"Is she dead?" I asked. Something in me spoke up. I guess I was being the strong one.

"No, she has very minimal brain function, but we still need to assess the situation. We need to find out how she got into this situation. The police will be called, and they'll investigate."

"Okay, cool." I heard hope in that statement, but I didn't want to be naïve. I knew her chances were slim.

My father just stood there with a blank look on his face. "Okay, let's go." He started walking before we could even say a word. He hopped in the car I came in, and I got in the passenger seat. Dre was in the other car, and he followed us until we got home. I went into the house while those two stayed outside talking. I walked into the room with the hot tub to look for anything that could help get to the bottom of this. I looked at the half-empty bottle of wine on the floor and then picked it up. I put it to my nostrils to take a sniff. I didn't know what I was looking at or for. I was just grasping at straws for reasons not to blame myself for what happened to my mother. I held on to the bottle and walked back toward the main part of the house; then I grabbed her cell phone off the table and went upstairs to my room. I didn't know what else to do.

"Corey!" I heard my father calling me from downstairs. I got up and walked down the stairs with an even face. Not happy or sad . . . just alive.

"Yes, sir?"

"We have to prepare for the worst. I'm going to be doing my own investigation. Fuck the police. I'm going to make a few calls and shut theirs down. Now, I need you to be in position. Trust no one."

"I already don't," I reassured him.

Chapter 59

Clayton

Agreement

Once again, we were sitting in the living room with the fireplace blazing. I was putting on the best performance of my life. My husband was sipping on a nice glass of Merlot while I just lingered in space.

I don't know what the hell I was waiting for. This love thing was complicated.

"So, are we ready to get this over with?" My husband, Anthony, looked at me with a somber and glazed look.

"What are you talking about?" I was confused.

"You're looking for my financier, aren't you?"

"I don't know what you're talking about." I needed more information before I was going to let on to my knowledge of anything.

"You're looking for the Ghost, right?"

"It's possible." I continued with my stance.

"Well, let's cut this Sherlock Holmes shit out and get down to it. This whole marriage is a setup, and you have a choice to make."

"A setup?" I asked with legitimate shock on my face.

"Yes. A fucking setup," he said, and then laughed. "You were duped."

"What?" I was a smart person, but this was crazy.

"I mean you are cute, and the dick was good, but you were supposed to be dead a long time ago. I convinced him to let you live for me. I like you, and you are easy. You some good arm candy. My friends love you. The Ghost, not so much."

"Dead?" I muttered to myself, but it was loud enough for him to hear it.

"Yes, adios, muchacho," he laughed.

"Bullshit. Ain't no way this is true," I said, still shrouded in disbelief.

"Dude, face it, you're not as smart as you think. You got got." He leaned back in his chair; then a smug smile covered his face.

"Ain't this a bitch." I shook my head, and then lowered it in shame.

"So the choice is yours. Join forces with me and help take over the city, or I can press one button on my cell phone and have some boys over here in seconds to scatter your body parts all over the city."

"*Those* are my choices?"

"Yes, that's it." He looked me straight in my eyes.

I looked back at him. He was such a fine brother and having all this luxury isn't too bad, either.

"This really isn't a real hard choice. You get to keep all of this and Ghost is willing to hand over the other guy you are looking for too. For free."

"Really?"

"Yes, really. He about to claim the whole city, and I'm here for the ride and the cash that goes with it. Aren't you tired of working for pennies? Aren't you tired of working—period?"

I sat there dumbfounded and confused. I had ethics. I was the guy that vowed to stop this and help the kids on the streets get out of the grip of this madness. Here I am contemplating joining forces with the other side.

"Fuck it. I am tired of struggling and scraping just to get by. I want to retire while I'm still young."

"Good. I was hoping that I didn't have to kill you and waste all that good meat between your legs. We'll continue to be a couple and be at our respective jobs until we get further instructions."

I nodded my head in agreement, but my mind was telling me to abort and run. I may have to play the double agent role and hope I make it out of this thing alive.

"Just so you know, if I even *feel* like you're lying, you will end up like my other walking Ken dolls around this city with only a flap and memories of a dick. I like my meat warm, so think twice about crossing me."

Chapter 60

Avery

Got 'Em

I just got off the phone with Anthony, and he got the detective to come under my umbrella of crime and leadership. It was nice to add him to my roster. I didn't trust him, though, as with most people, and for a minute, I didn't trust Anthony with getting Clayton to be in a relationship with him. Turns out that Anthony was good at getting Clayton to go along with the setup, which furthered my plans.

I was now on my way to the hospital to see poor Monica, who was unresponsive in a hospital bed. I had to go and play sympathetic when *I* was the reason she was there. If I wasn't a kingpin, acting probably would have been another vocation I would have excelled in. There still may be a chance. You never know.

I walked into the hospital with a sovereign attitude on the inside but a solemn look on the outside. I was feeling myself, and I was loving it as usual.

I smiled at a few people as I made my way over to the nurses' station to get Monica's room number.

"Good afternoon, beautiful. I'm here to visit a patient and need your expertise." My voice was low, yet still hypnotizing to the ear. The white nurse gushed with a smile on her face and then spoke after a second or two. I guess she had to get herself together. I understood. I probably would do that same thing in my presence.

"Patient's name?" she asked as she focused on my face. It was almost like I was a snake charmer, and she was the snake.

"Monica Grant."

"She's in room 302. Would you like me to escort you to the room?"

"No, that won't be necessary. But thank you for offer," I replied. I flashed my smile for her benefit before I turned on my heel and walked away.

It didn't take long for me to get to the room and open the door. The enemy was sitting in the seat next to her bed. He had his hand in hers.

Monica's body lay in the bed covered to the waist with a hospital sheet, but her upper torso was dressed very nicely. I assumed that Leroy had commissioned her to be that way.

"How are you holding up?" I greeted the faggot-hating drug supplier with a smile that said *I'm sorry you are here in this situation,* continuing my charade.

"As best as one can, given the situation." He looked a little worn, like he needed some rest.

"Any progress?"

"Nothing new. She's in the same state that she was in when she first arrived."

"Did they give you any indication of what might have caused this?" I already knew, but I wanted to see if he did as well.

"They're still running tests," he said, and then looked back at her. "She's a fighter, and this is just a test for both of us."

"Indeed, it is. I'm sure you all will be all right."

"I appreciate the encouragement. I'm worried about my son in all of this. He's close to his mother, and I don't know how he'll respond to this if it turns for the worst."

"Corey is a soldier. He'll be a trooper in all of this, I'm sure of it."

"I would agree to that as well."

Corey made his way into the room, and our attention was now focused on him and his presence.

"Good evening, Corey," I greeted him with my hand out ready for a handshake.

"Hey, Coach." He shook my hand, but there was some hesitancy there. He was probably still upset or disgruntled with the deal that I gave him, but I'll address it later.

"How are you holding up?" I asked, still pretending that I cared.

"I'm good." He let a smirk, which looked like a light smile, cover his face. He was acting as well.

Not too long after he came in, another person came in the room after him. It was his boyfriend, Dre. I had to admit that he was quite the looker, and he had a New York type swagger to him. He looked me up and down; then he went to stand beside Leroy. He was a threat to me, and I had no qualms with him. He was being loyal to his boss and doing what he was expected to do. I respected that.

Then a shocker walked through the door after that. The pretty chick that was playing the role of Corey's girlfriend walked in with a bright smile on her face and bouquet of flowers in her hand.

"Hello, everyone." She greeted us with a light and young voice.

Everyone spoke; then she made her way over beside Corey. She kissed him on the cheek, and then made her way to a chair not far from him.

I had to admit that Corey had this thing set up. I was impressed. He was fooling the masses with such ease. It made me proud.

I didn't stay long after the arrival of the extra people because I had other things to do and personas to be.

Chapter 61

Leroy

Fate

I couldn't bear the thought of losing my wife. She was the reason why I lived the life that I did. I played it strong in the head and on the outer, but my heart was breaking on the inside. I didn't want to lose my rib. Yes, I was tough and downright cruel to others, but I was a human, nonetheless.

My family is my world, especially my wife. I couldn't help but think that this is payback for all the wrong that I had done. But, even with all of that, I didn't think that I deserved this.

Losing my wife would be like losing my life. What would I live for? They say it takes drastic situations to change you, and I guess this is my turn. My fate. I don't want to bury my wife. I'm living the life running these streets.

It's supposed to be me in the bed not her. I did all the stickups, robberies, and murders to burn me in hell for eternity, and now I must sit here and bear this. It was torture, for sure. It's worse than anything my enemy could ever give to me.

Monica's brothers had been here and vowed to avenge her, and I was grateful. They were all loyal to me because of her and the great men in my army. Corey went to get something to eat. I, on the other hand, had no appetite. For food, that is.

I was alone in a room with just us two. I wanted to feel the warmth of her body wrapped around my own like when we slept in bed together. I was her protector, and she treated me as such. Now look at her.

I neglected her to build a kingdom for her, not knowing that she was my kingdom. All the stuff that I bought her and got for her wasn't what she wanted. She wanted me to spend time with her. She just wanted me. She turned to drinking for comfort, and now look at her.

Did it have to come to this to get my attention or the attention she needed and craved?

"Monica," I grabbed her hand and rubbed it. It was warm and soft as always. I lifted it up and put it to my nose. I could smell her sweet smell. It was the same smell from all those years ago when I met her. She was feisty and fiery when I met her. She was my soul mate, and we meshed from day one. And when she had our son, it solidified that love and admiration I had for her. She is stronger than I ever could be, and I needed her strength right now.

"Please don't leave me, girl. I love you, girl!" I moaned. Tears flowed freely from my eyes, and I didn't care about anything but her at the moment. I would give all the money I had just to hear her call my name, squeeze my hand, or anything that let me know she was still fighting for me—for us.

"Our son needs both his parents. We need you to come back. We're sorry we neglected you."

I held her hand in my own and let loose all the pain I was feeling on her shoulder.

Suddenly, I heard the door to the room open. I looked up and saw my son come in with some food in his hand. His little girlfriend was with him along with my boy Dre.

They all saw my tearstained face. I didn't care, though. It was what it was. I was not ashamed of the tears. I was ashamed of my actions before the tears.

Corey joined me at his mother's side while the others stood back and watched a family have its time together.

Chapter 62

Monica

Dreaming?

I can't feel nothing. But I can hear everything around me. Machines beeping and I know that my husband and son are in the room with me. I will my eyes to open, but nothing is happening. I can't feel anything. My body isn't responding to my begging and pleading.

Corey and Leroy are begging me to wake up, and I want to so badly, but it's not happening.

Please, God!

Please, God!

Am I dying?

Am I dead?

Is this a dream?

What's going on?

All I remember is drinking wine and sitting in the tub drifting and floating.

Now I'm here. Wherever *here* is.

All I wanted to do was ease the pain that I was in. I was lonely. The wine was my friend and companion. It made me not feel. Left me limp.

Where did I go wrong, God?

I was lost.

I was hurt.

Most of all, I was alone.

I was selfish too.

My husband and son were out there trying to provide a life for me, and I couldn't hold it together long enough to see it to the end. It wasn't going to be the way it was always.

Please, God, give me another chance!

I want my family.

I want to live.

I want to live.

I need to live.

Not for me but for them. They need me, and I need them.

Please, God!

Chapter 63

Corey

Drink Up

Seeing my father in the vulnerable state that he was in earlier was new for me. My mother was his everything, and you could tell by his tearstained face.

I came home while my father stayed at my mother's bedside. He told me to come home and make sure that business was being taken care of to his liking. Things happened so fast that it was unbelievable. He said that he would do everything to keep my mother here with us, but he wanted me to continue to lead the empire with the help of Dre.

I wasn't excited, but I held my first meeting in my father's absence, and it went better than I thought it would. They listened to me. I think that my father may have threatened them or something like that. I didn't think that I had that type of power, at least not yet. But Dre told me otherwise. He said that the power of my presence was there all along. I was an heir, and they treated me as such. My uncles were there as well, and that did help. I was running things in my father's absence, and I didn't want to fuck it up.

In the back of my mind, I still had the coach's plans too. He wanted me to hand over information as I got it. I didn't want to, but I did.

I dialed his number from my phone.

"Hello," he answered. His deep voice was a bit intimidating, but I moved past it because it was normal to me now.

"Hey, Coach." My voice was without enthusiasm or zeal.

"So I take it you have some information for me." Coach got right to the point. It's not like that wasn't normal for him.

"Yes, I do." I kept it short too. I wasn't in the mood for talking anyway. This was now a business relationship and no other. My respect for him was gone, and so was the trust.

I filled him in on the things I knew so far and felt a great bit of shame for turning over information to keep my secret safe. I felt like a bitch, and I didn't like that feeling at all.

"You've done good, Grasshopper. Talk to you soon," he said with a laugh and hung up the phone.

I was pissed at his happiness in a time when my family was suffering. This world was cruel and uncaring. I was starting to see that now. No one gave a fuck about anyone anymore. It's all about self-preservation.

I looked over to my nightstand and then went to pick up my mother's phone. I was amazed that it still powered on. I admired the picture she had on her screen. She is beautiful. She's sitting in a chair with one of her legs crossed with a flowered sundress on. It was outside on the gazebo, and the sun was shining on her in the right place. It was a perfect picture.

I didn't want to lose her.

I scrolled through her phone and looked at her phone log, and I saw nothing but Coach's number on the log the most except for me and my father and few others sprinkled throughout the list. This piqued my interest even more.

Then I scrolled through her messages to find the same thing. I was startled to see how many times she got a "treat" or a "gift" from Coach.

My antennae went up.

I called Dre.

"Dre, I need you at my house ASAP." I spoke with urgency.

"I got you. Give me a few. I'm with your pops right now. Be there in about a half."

"Cool." I hung up the phone and grabbed the bottle of wine that was left over from the other day.

I put it to my nose and began to sniff it. I didn't drink so I didn't know what I was looking for. I just knew that something wasn't right. My mother was a light drinker. Those text messages had addicted all over them.

It didn't take long for Dre to come over and talk. As soon as he came through the door, I said, "Coach has been supplying all the wine Mother drank, and from the text messages on her phone, there was a lot of drinking going on."

"So what do you want to do?" he asked, ready to do whatever for me. He was so fucking hot right now that I almost lost focus on the task at hand.

"I need to have one of our chemists break down this wine and see what's going on with it. It's not just a simple wine. My mother was an undercover fiend, and it's his fault. I know it. I just need proof."

"Damn," he shook his head. "This is some fucked-up shit."

Dre didn't know anything about the deal Coach and I had because it was on a need-to-know basis with me.

"Dre, call the chemist now and see how long it'll take to dissect this wine."

Dre pulled out his phone and immediately dialed a number. The conversation was short and to the point.

Turns out he could get the results back in one to two days. That was enough time for me.

All I had to do was play the part until I can figure out what I need to do next.

Two days later . . .

I now had the information that I needed. The wine that my mother was drinking was laced with promethazine, a highly addictive drug that was flooding the streets and can be laced with almost any drink and get you the high that you needed and craved. It was the one that Coach or Ghost was flooding the streets with and making him most of his money. I was fucking pissed, and I wanted to deal with him myself. I wanted kill this bitch dead. My mother is lying in a hospital bed close to death, and it was his fault. He knew what the fuck he was doing all along. This bitch had set all this up. We were pawns and didn't even know it.

I had been sitting by my mother's bedside hoping and praying with my father that she would wake up and things would go back to normal. But something told me that things would never be normal again.

My phone began to buzz. It was a text message from Coach.

"Dad, I need to make a call. I'll be right back." I tapped him on his shoulder. He had his head in my mother's lap, asleep, I assumed. I didn't want to wake him up, but I wanted to alert him of my movements.

He just nodded his head. It was a nice picture to see. I just wish it was under better circumstances.

I walked out of the room we were in and into another room. I made sure that it was empty and then closed the door so that I could get some privacy.

I dialed his number.

"The ball is moving, and you need to get your father out of the hospital and home," he ordered.

"Why?" I answered.

"That's none of your fucking business," he barked.

"He's not going to leave my mother's side for nothing. What do you want me to do?"

"Find a fucking way to get it done and make sure that he's alone when he goes. You don't want to break your father's heart even more by him finding out his best friend and his son are fucking like rabbits close to extinction."

He hung up the phone in my ear. I was pissed, and I didn't want to do it.

I walked back into the room, not knowing what to say or do or if I could even get my father to leave the hospital.

"Dad," I went over to him and shook him. He slowly lifted his head and looked at me.

"Dad, go home, shower, and change your clothes. You need it. Mom wouldn't want you here smelling as bad as you do." I smiled to try to ease the moment.

"Nah, I'm good, son." He lay his head back down.

"Dad, I'm serious." I shook him again. "I'll be here. It won't take you long to go and come back. Nothing is going to happen while you're gone. She would want you to." A few tears fell from my eyes as I mustered up the emotion that was sitting inside of me anyway.

"You sure?" he rose and looked at me.

"Dad, I want some time with her alone. That should be enough time."

"Okay, I'll do it only because I know that you're correct. She wouldn't want me all over her stinky. She did hate that." He had a small smile on his face. It was one that I hadn't seen in a while.

"Dad, if anything changes, you'll be the first to know. But I know that you'll be back in no time."

He gathered his things and hurried out of the room. I don't know what was going to happen, but I knew that it wasn't good. I just lay my head in the spot that my father just had his head and enjoyed the time alone with my mother as I said I would.

I texted Coach to let him know that my father had left and was headed home.

Chapter 64

Clayton

Kudos

I was sitting in my office waiting for my moment. I got information for the bust that was about to happen. Anthony came through for me, and I was having a change of heart. This was the moment I was waiting on. It just didn't happen the way I planned on it happening.

There was a knock on my door.

"Come in," I ordered.

"Detective, the task force is ready."

"Okay, I'm waiting on the call I need."

"Right." He nodded his head and then left.

Not more than a few seconds after that I received a text that I was waiting for.

We sat in the garage of one of his neighbors and watched as he parked his car. My heart raced at the sight of it all. This was the move of my career, and it was about to go down. I decided to wait until he got back in his car to leave, because that was where the drugs were planted. There were enough drugs in the trunk to get him jail time so that he would never see the light of day again.

It took about fifteen minutes for him to come out with a whole new outfit on, and as soon as he hopped in the car, I gave the signal, and we swarmed. He didn't even give up a fight when we threw him to the ground. It was like he knew that he wasn't guilty.

"We got you now. You're going to jail for a very long time," I whispered in his ear as they lowered him into the back of the unmarked car. We both watched as the drugs were taken out of his trunk. A look of shock covered his face. I think he knew that he was going down for a long time.

After it was all said and done, I received accolades from the chief of police, and I sat in my office thinking that it was all over after this because of my agreement with Anthony and joining the other side. I was going to be enabling evil. Willingly. That didn't sit right with me.

I went home. The home I shared with a man I loved and lusted after but hated what he does on the side for a living.

"Hey, baby, how was your day?" He greeted me with a kiss on the cheek. He knew how my day was. He was being cynical, and he knew it, but I went with it anyway.

I just smiled and went toward the kitchen. I was hoping that he was a good house husband and had a meal ready for me since he knew that I was on my way home anyway. I felt like a caged lion being poked. I didn't like it.

"I smell food. It smells good." I put on the act of a doting husband and sat down at the table.

"Congratulations are in order for the man of the hour. I couldn't wait until you got home to make you feel like the man that you are." Joy filled his words as he spoke.

He had my plate in the oven and pulled it out and set it in front of me. Then he removed the foil, and I saw a dinner fit for a king. I felt like it too. He grabbed his plate and sat down, and we ate together. He talked, I just listened. I didn't hear much of what he said because my morals were talking louder than anything now. He didn't stop talking, and I didn't stop eating.

Chapter 65

Avery

Checkmate

Three down and one to go.
Leroy "the competition"? Grant, incarcerated,
Clayton "the detective," food poisoning, dead.
Monica "the wife," vegetable, soon dead.
Now I was waiting to put my last piece of the puzzle in place.

This was the day that I was waiting for. I finally let Corey into the inner sanctum since he was now going to be handing over the other part of the city to me because he wants to live and he wants his lover to live. Besides, he didn't have a choice. It was mine anyway.

I sat at my desk as he was guided around the compound by one of my top men.

"So, did you like what you saw?" I asked him as he came into my private office that most don't get to see. He was a privileged individual right now. The only reason he was in this room with me is because he reminded me so much of myself. Right now, he was pissed that I had him in a tight spot and there was nothing that he could do about it. I let him meet with all my staff so that he could get used to the surroundings. I was going to offer him a spot on my team since he was in the game already. He was a fresh face and could add to my genius. Besides, I was molding him since day one to be a part of my team.

"Yes."

"That's all you're going to say?"

"What do you want me to say? I'm here against my will, and you want me to be happy about it. Man, fuck you and this."

I smiled at his tone. It was uncaring and quite daring. He was mad at the way things transpired, and I am not mad at him. I would be too.

"Corey, you are mad, and that's the way that I want you to be. I need you to be mad. This world will dick you around every time. Just be glad that I was the one and not one of the straight liars that pretend to like you and talk shit about you behind your back, waiting for an opportunity to show their true colors and stab you in the back."

"Fuck you mean? I should be *grateful* that you set my father up, and then addicted my mother to some damn drug that has her close to death right now? I should be fucking happy? *Happy?*"

He was right where I was when I was his age, and I could relate, except for the fact that both my parents are still alive, but we had the same story.

"You won't get this right now, and I'm not expecting you to do so. I just want you to be ruthless and heartless like most of the men. That's how they operate. I painfully snatched all my recruits off the streets, and now look at the dynasty that I've created. You should be grateful that I picked you. Your father got what he deserved. He got off easy. He could be dead right now. That's what I wanted to do, but I spared you because I liked you. Your mother was just a casualty of war. She wasn't happy anyway. I was helping her out of her misery. She killed herself. Just like any addict, they think they have it under control, only to end up worse off than before. You see, she was low before I got there. All she needed was something to get her higher. Just think, if your father wasn't busy chasing after a ghost, then your mother wouldn't have needed to be chasing the bottle. She put all her time and investment into her family and very little into herself. It didn't take long for me to come in and get her attention because she was thirsting like a vampire for blood. I just gave her a solution. What she did with it or what it did to her was her problem. You two were her drug of choice for so long; then you just dropped her. I only offered a viable replacement. You have yourselves to blame."

He sat there in silence. What could he say? I knew that I was right, and so did he. He had no choice but to agree with me.

"You're right. I should be grateful." He finally spoke up. I was glad that he agreed with me.

Chapter 66

Corey

All the King's Men

I sat at a long table that resembled one from a corporation board meeting. There were seven chairs that sat on both sides of the table. The room was decorated with a few celebrity pictures, mainly boxers and rap artists. My father loved boxing and rap in his spare time. There were two big-screen televisions on both walls opposite Dre and me.

I had a drink of liquor in front of me. Dre had a cigar that was burning in front of him. It was just me at one end and Dre at the other end. I was in one of my father's business buildings that had a disguise of a legitimate business in the front of it. There was an army waiting on us in cars. I looked at Dre in his eyes, and he did the same. Behind my eyes were thoughts of my father and my mother. Thoughts of the man that I trusted and was fooled by. There was some pain behind my eyes. I wanted to ball up in a fetal position and not get up. But I didn't cry. It would be a letdown for both of my parents. Neither one of them were weak or gave in easily. They were the epitome of strength. They made me who I was today. Dre looked fearless and ready to do what had to be done. I was glad to have him by my side. My ride or die, as they say.

"You ready to do this shit?" I asked Dre, and then gulped down the liquor I had in my glass. After that, I placed the glass back on the table. It made a noise as it hit the table that echoed throughout the room.

"My hands been itching for a minute now. I have payback on my mind. He did my peoples dirty, so now I must return some dirt back to his front door. Oh yeah, I'm *ready* for this shit." He puffed on his cigar a couple more times after he talked, and then put it out in the ashtray.

I stood up, then he followed suit. Dre was dressed up like he worked for the police task force. I've seen him in action before, and I trusted him with my back.

"Let's go get this muthafucka!"

I exited the room, and he followed me a few minutes later. I hopped in the car and made my way to the destination I was headed to. Dre had all the information that I had, so he followed me along with trucks that had a small army spread throughout them. I'm sure that there would be casualties on both sides. I prayed that it wasn't Dre or myself. We planned how we thought it would, and should, go and had plans if it didn't. I just prayed that I didn't die trying to avenge my family. And if Dre died, I would truly be lost. I mean, I have my uncles on my mother's side, but I wasn't as close to them as I was with Dre. I pulled up to my destination, and then breathed in and let it out.

"This is it," I said, and then got out of the car.

"You know, Coach, I'm so glad that you picked me because I didn't know what to do with this life, and I wasn't sure until a few days ago. I want to be a kingpin. I want what you have. I want what my father gave me, and I'm not going to just hand it over to you like you thought I would. You say I should be afraid of you, and for a long time, I was. But what was I afraid of? You? Nah, you don't exist. You're a ghost, remember? You're dead to this world and to all the people that you mattered to when you were born. So right now, I'm going to give *you* a choice. Do you want to live or die?"

He laughed at me before he spoke, but that was cool. He didn't take me seriously, and most wouldn't since I'm just a young black dude needing something to do with his life.

"You had it all figured out about me and my family, right? We were sitting ducks waiting to be taken out. Now, you're looking at me with a smile on your face, and you're probably thinking that I'm crazy too. I was a pawn to you. A come up, as we young people say. Not anymore. How about you were the pawn *I* was looking for? You have a ready-made kingdom for the taking. All because I reminded you of yourself. Ha! All I have to do is unite the two and have my way." I laughed at the now-serious look on his face.

"You have lost your fucking mind if you think that you can, and will, sit in my presence and talk to me like that. All it takes is one button and you're dead. My men will swarm in like locusts."

"You think so? I would check that fact first. Go ahead and push the button . . . and see who dies," I dared him. He pushed a button on his desk . . . but nothing happened. I knew that it wouldn't. His men, now *my* men, were long gone. You see, most people are only loyal to themselves in the end. And when you throw in more of what they are getting from one man, they almost immediately reconsider their options. Guns in their faces and a few dead comrades in front of them doesn't help either. They say money is a motivator, and it worked very well with many of these guys. I gave them options of getting out and some left, but the majority had nowhere else to go. A sad reality is that Ghost used these guys' desperation and hopelessness to fuel his empire, and it worked. That is not how I wanted to run my empire. Willing workers have less of a chance of doing you dirty. Of course, there will be ones who try. It comes with the territory.

"I don't hear anyone coming. Does it usually take that long for results with you?" I said and then laughed.

He looked furious, but he didn't say a thing.

"What the fuck is going on?" he hopped out of his chair and lunged toward me. Just before he got to me, the door to his office burst open and Dre came in with his gun in hand. One shot to the arm propelled Coach backward and to the floor.

"That was cutting it close, Dre. This bitch was about to off my ass."

"I got this, babe." He leaned in and kissed me on the lips. It was our first kiss in front of someone else. It was powerful at that very moment, but I was concentrated on the task at hand.

"You fucking ingrate. I trusted you. I *made* you. You were just a faggot playing sports, and I picked your ass up and dusted you off. You won't be able to handle this city like I was going to. You too weak. Just like your father. Look at you and this punk bitch acting like you all in love. Love is a weakness."

"Shut up, bitch. How the fuck do you know about love when you gave up on it so early on? You never gave it a chance. You were already loved the day you were born. You just wanted it the way you wanted it, and no other way. You saw some images that you didn't like it and created a war on a world that doesn't care about anyone other than itself. That's why I'm going to give it all that it wants, one person at a time. I'm going with the flow of the world.

"Pick this piece of shit up off the floor," I instructed a few of the men that followed Dre in here. They did as they were instructed and placed him in the chair that he was originally sitting in.

"So this is how this is going to play out. I'm going to repeat this nursery rhyme to you and see if you can follow where I'm going with this. Ready?

"Humpty Dumpty sat on a wall, Humpty Dumpty had a great fall. All the king's horses and all the king's men couldn't put Humpty together again. You see were I'm going with this yet?"

"Fuck you," he spat in my direction.

"Okay, so you *do* get it. Every king has a high time and a low time. A wall and a fall. You had your wall and now your fall. And your men are surrounded by mine, so they can't help you. Now, I'm going to have you dismembered and spread out all over the city as retribution for your crimes. I've always loved that nursery rhyme. Never thought that I would have to use it in such a way, though." I laughed. He looked pissed. He had it all worked out except for the end. We never do.

Epilogue

Corey

Who would have thought that I would be running a drug and crime empire in the city of Baltimore at such a young age? This is the thought that I was having sitting in an auditorium waiting to graduate from high school. I wasn't a ghost per se, but I wasn't open with my business either. I had to admit that I was still learning, but with what I learned from watching my father and the things that Dre was teaching me, I was coming along quite nicely. My father's men instantly became my men upon his imprisonment, and it flowed smoothly. I also had men from Coach come on board with me. I had a meeting with my expectations in place and hopes that we can get along without sexuality issues and egos coming into play. I wasn't forcing anyone to stay, and I wasn't making anyone leave. I demanded appreciation for what every individual brought to the table and respect for differences. Be who you are and live your life. I was the boss, but I was open to suggestions that could make us all richer.

"Corey Grant," I heard my name being called, so I got up and crossed the stage to collect my diploma. You see, I continued my life in high school and was graduating with honors. My parents would be proud of me. I looked in the crowd and found Dre with a smile on his face. He was a great supporter and helped me make some tough decisions over the last year. Like taking my mother off life support and watching her take her last breath. I was heartbroken and still angry at how it all played out, but I was okay with it now. I still had my father, even though he will never see the streets again. I had Coach to thank for all of that. I still had Diana, my decoy, in place. She was in the loop about things now, though. I still had to play the part in the streets, even though what I did for a living wasn't on public display. My father always said there is always someone looking for the next come up, even if it means killing you to get it. I get what Coach was doing by remaining anonymous, but I didn't want to live my life as a recluse and unlovable. I believed in love. I didn't choose this life; it chose me. I believe that. I don't want this drug game to change me, but I believe that it would. I just hope that it is for my good. The reality of me supplying this city with drugs and such weighs on me at times, but I just move past it. I'm a businessman just like the owner of McDonald's. We are both supplying a need. It's just to different clientele and under different circumstances. That's my logic, and I am sticking with it.